KT-552-522

MORE TALES OF HOFFMAN

MARTIN HOFFMAN

faber and faber
LONDON·BOSTON

First published in 1983
by Faber and Faber Limited
3 Queen Square, London WC1N 3AU
Filmset by Wilmaset
Birkenhead, Merseyside
Printed in Great Britain by
The Thetford Press
Thetford, Norfolk
All rights reserved

© *Martin Hoffman, 1983*

CONDITIONS OF SALE

This book is sold subject to the condition that it shall not, by way of trade or
otherwise, be lent, resold, hired out or otherwise circulated without the
publisher's prior consent in any form of binding or cover other than that in
which it is published and without a similar condition including
this condition being imposed on the subsequent purchaser

British Library Cataloguing in Publication Data

Hoffman, Martin
  More tales of Hoffman
  1. Contract bridge
  I. Title
  795.41'5   GV1282.3

  ISBN 0-571-13146-8
  ISBN 0-571-13187-5 Pbk

Library of Congress Data has been applied for

Contents

Acknowledgements

Once again I am much indebted to Gus Calderwood, captain of the British team in the 1981 World Championship, for reading the typescript of this book and for making many helpful suggestions; to my wife, Audrey, for her assistance in preparing the typescript; and to the editors of Faber and Faber for reshaping my imperfect English.

More of my Ideas on Bridge

In the introduction to my first book I made some general points about my ideas on the game, and one or two of these I would like to repeat.

'It is right to be busy when the outcome of a hand is in doubt, but wrong to enter when it is clear that the opponents are going to obtain the final contract.'

'Your aim in a big pairs event must be high but it must also be steady. You can win with several average scores and a fair number of good scores that will come quite naturally.'

Those two considerations arise time and again in this book. Here are some more of my general theories:

Opening leads

In general, both at rubber bridge and in competitions, I aim to make the obvious opening lead. At rubber bridge I don't want to destroy my partner's confidence. I may think another lead would be better, but I don't want the situation to arise in which partner will say (or at any rate think): 'If Martin had made the obvious lead we would have beaten the contract. These good players are all the same, they must try to be clever.' If your partner has confidence in you he will let you take control and he will play his best with you. Of course, I do sometimes make an irregular lead, but only when I am sure there is a good case for it. I had an example the other day when I held as West:

♠ 10 x x
♡ K J x x x x
♢ x x
♣ Q x

11

The final contract was four spades. North, on my left, had bid diamonds and clubs. I thought we would make only one trick in hearts at most, and to keep the lead I began with the *king* of hearts. This held the trick, and when I saw the dummy it was easy to switch to the queen of clubs. We made two club tricks and a third club promoted a trump trick.

It is the same at duplicate. I like to make the same lead as the rest of the field, trusting my side to play a little better than the rest thereafter.

One other point: I seldom underlead aces—only just enough to keep regular opponents guessing. Also, I am seldom misled by an opponent who leads low through a suit bid by dummy. It is far more likely that the lead is from A x x than from Q x x.

Gadgets

I am not a 'gadget' man. Sometimes you will see two players at the beginning of a pairs session telling one another all their favourite gadgets, and down they go on the convention card. How ridiculous this is! If you are playing a system such as the Blue Club you must know what you are doing, it is true, but it is a mistake to superimpose on your system a host of artificial bids or sequences. How many times have you heard even very good players saying after a session 'I forgot that my partner's bid meant . . .'? Apart from the danger of failing to remember, I for one find the game difficult enough without placing extra strain on my concentration.

Partners

At rubber bridge it is essential for weak partners to think you are happy to cut them. Just as all 24-handicap golfers think they are better than other 24-handicap players, so poor bridge players believe they play a reasonable game, and if you seem to share that view you will get the best out of them.

Generally speaking, I don't offer advice or criticism unless I am asked. The important thing is to meet partner on his own ground. If he is a bad player, say what he might have done and he will think he's learned something. If a fairly good player has made a mistake, he probably knows it, and you mustn't be insincere.

Playing bad hands

Sometimes opponents will bid a slam and you will have what seems to be a valueless hand. Obviously, you mustn't appear to be disinterested. It is as important at bridge as at poker to keep a 'poker face'. Also, don't make the mistake of thinking that because you hold a bad hand you can relax. I remember once, when I was playing for quite a high stake, I held as West:

> ♠ K J 9 x x
> ♡ x
> ♢ 9 8
> ♣ K 10 x x x

South played in 6NT after I had made an overcall of one spade. I led the 9 of diamonds and it soon became clear that declarer had 11 tricks on top and that I was in danger of being end-played. Since I had not mentioned my clubs, my plan was to come down to the singleton king of spades and K 10 x of clubs. If the declarer read me for 6–4 and tried a throw-in with ace and another club, I would surprise him by producing an unexpected club. But alas, my partner, who had begun with 6 5 2 of spades, discarded the 2 and the 5 early on. Taking note of this, the declarer dropped my king of spades. 'I wanted to show you how many spades I had,' said East. On such occasions you must trust your partner to know what is happening and not inform the declarer.

Tempo

A very slow player may be a good player, but if he could speed up he would be much better. When you have a difficult hand to play it is right to take your time when the dummy goes down. At this stage the declarer, with a sight of two hands in partnership, has a big advantage over the defenders. Once you have formed a plan, carry it out with fair speed. It is true that in this book I describe some quite difficult hands, where the declarer must pause to work out the best line; but against this, there are hundreds of contracts which you will make simply because the defence has been weak.

Some good players, in a more or less hopeless contract, will start a fast rap-rap, as though there were nothing to think about. Whether this is entirely fair or not is a moot point. At any rate, if my partner is not a strong player and may have problems, I deliberately slow down the play so that he will have time to think.

Those little hesitations

Although most books don't say much about it, every rubber bridge player knows what an important part is played by small hesitations. I wouldn't like to be thought of as a 'sharp' player, but at the same time I don't want other players to be sharp at my expense. So I pay a good deal of attention to the habits of my opponents. Take a situation of this sort:

A 10 x x

K J 9 x

You lead the jack from hand. The clubs are full of players who, holding x x x, will give it just a tiny hesitation. They are not, in their own minds, being in the least unfair: they think they are just protecting themselves. You may be caught out once by such tactics, but don't give any indication and from then on you will always do the right thing against this opponent.

Points are only—points

Learning a point count is helpful to beginners. Thereafter points are a snare and a delusion. You will hear a player who has opened some wretched 4–3–3–3 12-count, vulnerable, say 'I had to open, I had 12 points.' Remember that points are at best a guide, a quick way of summarizing high cards. They must never determine your call. If you have a fit with partner the value of your hand is increased. If not, it is decreased.

It's all in the mind

When a good player makes a mistake it's a wrong view. When a lesser player does the same thing, it's a blunder.

1 Second Best

Your side is not vulnerable, partner opens one club, the next player doubles and you hold:

♠ 8 6 3
♡ K J 7 6 4
♢ —
♣ K 10 8 6 3

What would you say now? There are several possibilities. You could pre-empt in clubs, but the objection to this is that partner's one club might be a prepared bid on a three-card suit. Also, how high do you go? You might bid one heart, intending to support clubs later. However, if you do this, partner may suspect that your heart response was psychic. I decided at the table to bid two hearts, which I play as forcing for one round. The bidding continued:

South	West	North	East
—	—	1♣	dble
2♡	No	4♡	No
No	No		

West led the queen of diamonds and this dummy went down:

                    ♠ A Q 9
                    ♡ A 10 9 5
                    ◇ 9 8 4
                    ♣ A Q 4
    ◇ Q led
                    ♠ 8 6 3
                    ♡ K J 7 6 4
                    ◇ —
                    ♣ K 10 8 6 3

It is always important, in pairs, to consider the likely contract at other tables. Obviously six hearts is a good contract here, especially if played by North. The slam might be reached if North opened a strong notrump (South a transfer 2◇, North 2♡, South 4◇, indicating a void). However, I was playing in a heat of the Philip Morris and it seemed to me that the majority of the field would fail, as we had done, to reach any slam. I thought that if I could make a trick more than most of the others in four hearts I would still obtain a fair score.

It was reasonable to assume that the diamonds would be 5–5 and that East, who had doubled the opening one club, would hold the queen of hearts. I could see chances of making a lot of tricks on a reverse dummy, but because of the entry position I would have to take certain risks.

After ruffing the diamond lead I crossed to the ace of clubs and ran the 10 of hearts from dummy. If I was going to ruff three times in my own hand, this first-round finesse was essential. When the 10 held I ruffed another diamond. This left:

♠ A Q 9
♡ A 9 5
◇ 9
♣ Q 4

♠ 8 6 3
♡ K J
◇ —
♣ K 10 8 6

Still playing for the maximum, I led a club to dummy's queen. This might have been ruffed, but the trick would come back because my last trump would be available for a diamond ruff and I would still make the long club in my own hand. As it turned out, East followed to the second club. I then ruffed dummy's third diamond, cashed the king of hearts, and returned to dummy to draw the last trump. So I ended with thirteen tricks—four hearts in dummy, three ruffs, five clubs and the ace of spades. The full hand was:

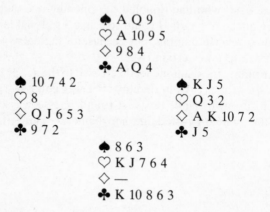

♠ A Q 9
♡ A 10 9 5
◇ 9 8 4
♣ A Q 4

♠ 10 7 4 2
♡ 8
◇ Q J 6 5 3
♣ 9 7 2

♠ K J 5
♡ Q 3 2
◇ A K 10 7 2
♣ J 5

♠ 8 6 3
♡ K J 7 6 4
◇ —
♣ K 10 8 6 3

Since few pairs reached a slam, making three overtricks produced a good score. If the second club had been ruffed I would have made my contract and players in six hearts would have been defeated.

1. Many players treat a jump by the opener's partner after a take-out double as a weak pre-empt, on a suit such as Q J 9 x x x. In my experience this type of bidding is more helpful to the doubling side than to anyone else.

2. It is always advisable, when the dummy goes down, to consider whether you are in a good, normal, risky, or poor contract. On the present deal I felt that most players would be in four hearts, so I aimed to make as many tricks as possible. If I had thought that the majority would be in a slam I would have played for a bad distribution of clubs and hearts, as this would have been the only way to obtain a good score.

2 Bracing Air

Perhaps because of the bracing air, I always find interesting deals when I play at the Swiss resort of Crans-sur-Sierre. Here is a defence played by the Pakistani champion, Zia Mahmood:

```
              ♠ K 7 6
              ♡ A 10
              ◇ A 8 7 6
              ♣ 10 8 7 2
                             ♠ Q J 10 5
                             ♡ K Q J
      ◇ J led                ◇ K 3 2
                             ♣ K 9 3
```

East-West were vulnerable and South was the dealer. The bidding went:

South	West	North	East
1♠	No	2♣	No
3♣	No	3♠	No
4♠	No	No	No

West led the jack of diamonds, declarer played low from dummy, and the king won. As East, what would you lead now? Oh well, don't tell me, because I think I know: you would place the king of hearts on the table, and so would almost everyone else. But Zia returned the 9 of clubs. See the effect of that:

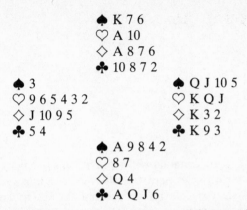

```
              ♠ K 7 6
              ♡ A 10
              ◇ A 8 7 6
              ♣ 10 8 7 2
♠ 3                         ♠ Q J 10 5
♡ 9 6 5 4 3 2               ♡ K Q J
◇ J 10 9 5                  ◇ K 3 2
♣ 5 4                       ♣ K 9 3
              ♠ A 9 8 4 2
              ♡ 8 7
              ◇ Q 4
              ♣ A Q J 6
```

When the 9 of clubs came back at trick two, the declarer thought, 'That might be a singleton. I won't risk a ruff, I'll go up with the ace and hope to lose just one spade, one club and one diamond.' The result was one down.

Of course it was plain to East that his side would not make a trick in hearts. The declarer was likely to hold only four red cards and would be able to dispose of his second heart on the ace of diamonds.

POINTS TO REMEMBER

1. The return of the 9 of clubs worked here because the declarer did not know that the trumps were breaking 4–1. A defender who has an unexpected trick either in the trump suit or a critical side suit can often persuade the declarer to make a false safety play before he knows about the distribution of the main suits.

2. Was it reasonable play on the declarer's part to go up with the ace of clubs at trick two? I would say yes, against any average opposition. But when you are playing in a pairs and your opponent is a top-class player, you should normally not be deflected from the natural line of play. Suppose, here, that the club *had* been a singleton; in that case the player obtaining the ruff would probably be the one with the longer trumps. In general, you mustn't allow a clever opponent to trick you into following an unlikely line of play.

3 Please Take

One of these days someone will write a complete book on the subject of loser-on-loser play, because the variations seem to be endless. This deal was played in a match at the Stefan's and Acol club in north London:

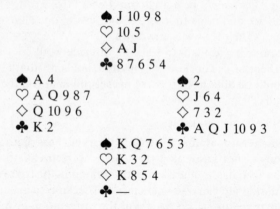

```
                    ♠ J 10 9 8
                    ♡ 10 5
                    ◇ A J
                    ♣ 8 7 6 5 4
♠ A 4                                    ♠ 2
♡ A Q 9 8 7                              ♡ J 6 4
◇ Q 10 9 6                               ◇ 7 3 2
♣ K 2                                    ♣ A Q J 10 9 3
                    ♠ K Q 7 6 5 3
                    ♡ K 3 2
                    ◇ K 8 5 4
                    ♣ —
```

West was the dealer at love all and the bidding at my table went like this:

South	West	North	East
—	1♡	No	2♣
2♠	3◇	4♠	5♣
5♠	dble	No	No
No			

Obviously five clubs can be beaten by a diamond lead and

return, but if South makes the more natural lead of the king of spades the contract will depend on how the hearts are played.

West led the king of clubs against five spades doubled. I ruffed and led a low spade. To avoid being left on play at a later stage, West went up with the ace and exited with his second spade. I won in hand, finessed the jack of diamonds and cashed the ace. After a club ruff the position was:

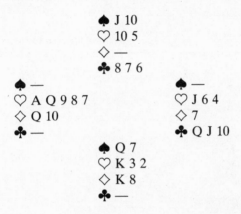

I led the king of diamonds, discarding a heart from dummy, and another diamond, on which I threw the remaining heart. Now West was left on play.

At the other table South played in five spades undoubled. I don't know exactly how the play went, but the endgame was the same as shown above. South discarded a heart on the king of diamonds, then made the mistake of ruffing his last diamond. East had the good sense to cover the 10 of hearts and the declarer finished a trick short.

POINTS TO REMEMBER

1. Note that at both tables West avoided the trap of leaving himself with the singleton ace of trumps. A defender who holds Ax in the trump suit must always be wary of ducking the first round, because a player who leaves himself with the singleton ace of trumps is often exposed to an end play.

2. When the declarer at the other table ruffed the fourth diamond he was no doubt thinking, 'If I can run the 10 of hearts to the West hand, West will be left on play.' Of course, it was better to let West hold the fourth round of diamonds. The moral is that, so far as possible, a declarer should not attach his mind to a particular line of play until he has considered the alternatives.

4   Early Decision

With neither side vulnerable the bidding begins:

South	West	North	East
—	—	—	1◇
dble	No	?	

Sitting North, you hold:

♠ K J 8
♡ Q 6 2
◇ K Q 10 7 5 3
♣ 9

In match play I would certainly pass, expecting to take 300 or so. At pairs the decision is more difficult, because 300 won't compensate for a missed game. At other tables the bidding may not go the same way and you may find that there is an easy game your way. As I don't like to 'take a view' on the first round of the auction, I responded two diamonds. This was the full hand:

                    ♠ K J 8
                    ♡ Q 6 2
                    ◇ K Q 10 7 5 3
                    ♣ 9

♠ 10 6 4   ♠ A 7 3
♡ 9 7   ♡ 10 4 3
◇ 6 4   ◇ A J 9 2
♣ K 7 6 5 4 3   ♣ A Q 8

                    ♠ Q 9 5 2
                    ♡ A K J 8 5
                    ◇ 8
                    ♣ J 10 2

The bidding went:

South	West	North	East
—	—	—	1◇
dble	No	2◇	No
2♡	No	3♡	No
4♡	No	No	No

This was a borderline contract, obviously, but if West makes
the normal lead of a diamond declarer has no great problem.
However, West chose the awkward lead of a trump. Declarer can
still play for a club ruff, but the defenders will lead another heart
and South won't have time to establish a diamond winner before
he has lost two clubs, a spade and a diamond.

After the trump lead my partner began quite rightly with a
diamond to the king and ace. When East returned a second
trump, South won and led a spade to the king. East won with the
ace and led a third round of trumps, producing this position:

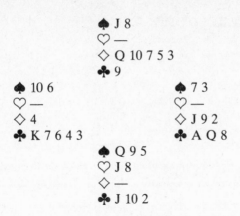

```
              ♠ J 8
              ♡ —
              ◇ Q 10 7 5 3
              ♣ 9
♠ 10 6                      ♠ 7 3
♡ —                        ♡ —
◇ 4                        ◇ J 9 2
♣ K 7 6 4 3                ♣ A Q 8
              ♠ Q 9 5
              ♡ J 8
              ◇ —
              ♣ J 10 2
```

In dummy after the third heart, South cashed the queen of diamonds, ruffed a diamond, and led a low spade. When West played low, declarer finessed the 8, ruffed another diamond, and returned to ♠J to make two more diamond tricks. Thus he made the contract, losing just one spade, one diamond and one club.

POINTS TO REMEMBER

1. Had I held, as North, a singleton in one of the majors and three clubs, I would have passed the double of one diamond, as our hands might well have been a misfit. As things were, I didn't want to risk missing game in a major suit. The tactical point is that it is dangerous to take critical decisions on the first round of the auction.

2. As perhaps you noticed, neither the declarer nor the defenders played perfectly. In the second diagram West should have inserted the 10 of spades to block the finesse. Most players have read about this sort of position but consistently miss it in the play. South could have forestalled this defence by leading the 9 of spades on the first round of the suit.

5 The Exception

Some forms of play almost always look right and generally are right—but not always. Consider this deal from rubber bridge:

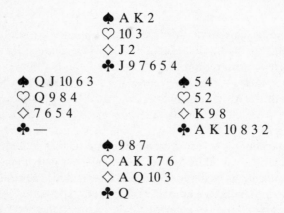

♠ A K 2
♡ 10 3
♢ J 2
♣ J 9 7 6 5 4

♠ Q J 10 6 3
♡ Q 9 8 4
♢ 7 6 5 4
♣ —

♠ 5 4
♡ 5 2
♢ K 9 8
♣ A K 10 8 3 2

♠ 9 8 7
♡ A K J 7 6
♢ A Q 10 3
♣ Q

West was the dealer at love all and after two passes East opened one club. The bidding continued:

South	West	North	East
—	No	No	1♣
dble	1♠	2NT	No
4♡	dble	No	No
No			

North's 2NT was exaggerated—a free bid of 1NT would have been sufficient. South's jump to four hearts was also unsound. West led the queen of spades and when East saw the dummy he was not at all happy, since at least one of his high cards was going to be wasted. The declarer won the spade lead in dummy and followed with the jack of diamonds. East covered, South won and cashed two more diamonds. The positions was then:

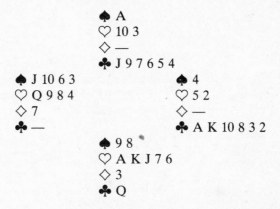

```
                    ♠ A
                    ♡ 10 3
                    ◇ —
                    ♣ J 9 7 6 5 4
♠ J 10 6 3                          ♠ 4
♡ Q 9 8 4                          ♡ 5 2
◇ 7                                ◇ —
♣ —                                ♣ A K 10 8 3 2
                    ♠ 9 8
                    ♡ A K J 7 6
                    ◇ 3
                    ♣ Q
```

South ruffed his fourth diamond with the 10 of hearts and East slyly discarded his remaining spade. Slyly, but unwisely. South followed with ace and king of hearts, then led the queen of clubs. East, who had nothing but clubs left, was suddenly in trouble. If he continued with a high club he would set up the jack in dummy, and if he played a low club declarer would simply discard his losing spade.

So you see, East's discard of a spade when the fourth diamond was ruffed was not so clever as he thought.

POINTS TO REMEMBER

1. It is strange how players with a strong holding in a suit that has been doubled for take-out will overbid. To hold something like K J 9 x in a suit that has been opened on your left is no great asset: those high cards will not pull their usual weight.

2. East's discard of a spade in the diagram position just *looked* pretty. A little thought would have shown that it could achieve nothing here and might be a mistake.

29

6 Shoot to Kill

You will always find a cosmopolitan field in a Swiss tournament. On the present occasion Nuri Pakzad, of Iran, was partnered by the Israeli internationai, Schmuel Lev.

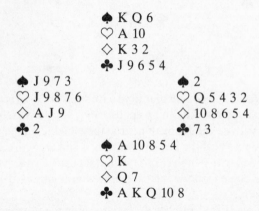

North was the dealer at game all. Six clubs is an easy contract, obviously. Some pairs tried for a better score in six spades, but this was bound to fail after the lead of the ace of diamonds. When Nuri held the South cards the bidding went like this:

South	North
—	1♣
2♠	3♠
4NT	5♦
6NT	No

South took the view, quite reasonably, that if the spades were solid there would be twelve tricks in notrumps as well as in spades or clubs. If there was a gap in the spades, then there would be better chances in 6NT than in six of the suit.

West led a low heart, won by the declarer's king. Nuri crossed to the king of spades and followed with the queen. When East showed out, the declarer realized that he still had a chance so long as West held the ace of diamonds in addition to his spades. The first move was to cross to the ace of clubs and lead a low diamond, which West could not afford to win. South soon arrived at this position:

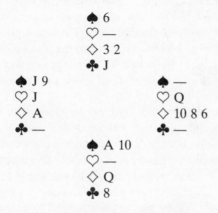

The last club was led and after throwing the jack of hearts on this trick West was end-played.

POINTS TO REMEMBER

1. In a pairs event good players always have their eye on 6NT, not only because it scores better than six of a suit but because it is not exposed to such accidents as an early ruff.

2. It would have been slightly better, perhaps, to lead a low diamond to the king at trick two. This is the best way to sneak thirteen tricks if the spades break, and if West holds four spades and the ace of diamonds the end play will still work as on the actual deal.

7 Valuable Discard

One day I was discussing with some friends which country produces the best bridge players. The question needs to be defined a little more closely. If you were to ask which country had the best two hundred players you have to say America, because they have so many very good players. The best eight players? At one time Britain would have come into the reckoning but now, I suppose, Italy, with Belladonna, Garozzo, Forquet and Franco to lead the way, must come first. Then France and America, about equal.

But what country could field the strongest fifty players—or perhaps I should say, the strongest twenty-five pairs? The answer, I am sure, is Poland. Polish pairs are always at the top in the Philip Morris tournaments in Europe, and many of the top players in other countries, especially Israel, are of Polish origin. They have an advantage over pairs from America and elsewhere in that the systems they play are not subject to the same kind of restrictions. A pair that has a host of artificial bids is difficult to play against, and the systems have technical advantages as well.

One of the many fine Polish players in London, Marius Wlodarczyk, noted a most unusual situation on this deal from the Spring Foursomes at Eastbourne:

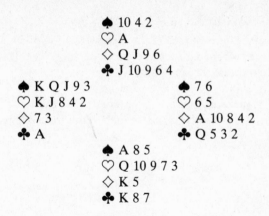

```
              ♠ 10 4 2
              ♡ A
              ◇ Q J 9 6
              ♣ J 10 9 6 4
♠ K Q J 9 3                    ♠ 7 6
♡ K J 8 4 2                    ♡ 6 5
◇ 7 3                          ◇ A 10 8 4 2
♣ A                            ♣ Q 5 3 2
              ♠ A 8 5
              ♡ Q 10 9 7 3
              ◇ K 5
              ♣ K 8 7
```

North-South did well with a modern type of sequence:

South	West	North	East
1♡[1]	1♠	dble[2]	No
2♣[3]	No	No[4]	No

[1]Precision system, indicating a five-card suit and a limited hand.

[2]A negative double, asking partner to describe his hand further.

[3]With this distribution the opener bids his lower minor.

[4]Wisely judging that game is unlikely.

Sitting West, Marius led the king of spades. South won and advanced the king of diamonds. East might have let this hold, but he preferred to win and lead a second spade. On the third spade he discarded a diamond. The declarer now made eight tricks quite easily, losing two spades, a diamond and two trumps.

West now suggested that his partner would have done better to discard a heart on the third round of spades. The defence then plays a fourth spade. Suppose, first, that South ruffs in dummy with ♣9 and East discards his remaining heart. South runs the jack of clubs to the ace, a heart is ruffed, and though declarer can pick up the remaining trumps he must lose another trick and go one down.

33

Perhaps South should take the spade ruff in his own hand, East again discarding a heart? It looks now as though the defence should take two spades, ace and queen of clubs, a heart ruff, and ace of diamonds, for one down.

So can South make the contract against this defence? Try discarding the ace of hearts from dummy on the fourth spade! East discards his second heart and South ruffs, leaving this position:

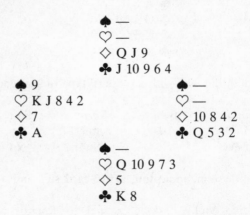

Now the declarer can cross to ◇Q and play a club to the 8 and ace. He must still play carefully to avoid a trump promotion.

POINTS TO REMEMBER

1. Most players are nervous of conceding a ruff and discard, but when the declarer has no loser to discard this form of play will often produce an unexpected trick.

2. Should West begin an echo in diamonds when the king is led? Should East play high-low in hearts? Players usually do, but when you have a good partner, capable of drawing inferences from the declarer's play, it is far better not to inform the world of your distribution.

8 On Show

As often happens, East's use of the unusual 2NT was helpful to the opposition on this deal:

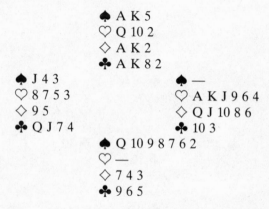

```
                    ♠ A K 5
                    ♡ Q 10 2
                    ◇ A K 2
                    ♣ A K 8 2
♠ J 4 3                             ♠ —
♡ 8 7 5 3                           ♡ A K J 9 6 4
◇ 9 5                               ◇ Q J 10 8 6
♣ Q J 7 4                           ♣ 10 3
                    ♠ Q 10 9 8 7 6 2
                    ♡ —
                    ◇ 7 4 3
                    ♣ 9 6 5
```

I held the South cards at rubber bridge and was pleased to hear my partner open two clubs. Neither side was vulnerable and East came in with 2NT. I thought it advisable to pass for the moment and the bidding continued:

South	West	North	East
—	—	2♣	2NT
No	3♣	dble	3♡
3♠	No	3NT	4◇
4♠	No	5♠	No
6♠	No	No	No

My partner bid his hand well, I thought. West led the 8 of hearts. I ruffed and drew trumps, East discarding two hearts and one diamond. I could see eleven tricks, but where was the twelfth to come from? Obviously East held the length in hearts and diamonds, but I could see no way to squeeze him.

What about the clubs? It looked as though East was 0–6–5–2, and West, with ♣ Q J 10 x, might have led the queen of clubs. So perhaps East had a doubleton with one of the honours?

Having reached this conclusion, I made the rather unusual play of a low club from the table. The 9 lost to the queen (big deception!) and West exited with a diamond. The position now was:

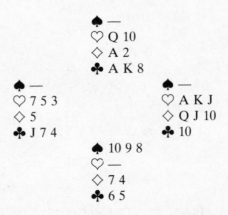

I cashed the king of clubs, ruffed a heart, and finessed the 8 of clubs with a fair degree of confidence.

1. The lead of the low club from dummy to establish a finessing position was unusual. Fortunately East had given me an exact picture of his distribution.

2. My partner asked me whether I had thought of playing a trump squeeze. If West had led a spade or a club, this would have been a possible line of play. Declarer gives up a club and aims for this type of ending:

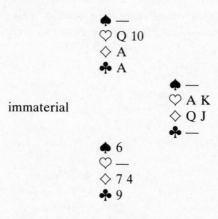

```
              ♠ —
              ♡ Q 10
              ◇ A
              ♣ A
                          ♠ —
                          ♡ A K
  immaterial              ◇ Q J
                          ♣ —

              ♠ 6
              ♡ —
              ◇ 7 4
              ♣ 9
```

Now a club to the ace squeezes East. After a heart lead this ending is impossible, because the defenders can lead a second heart when in with a club.

9 Plain Features

Sometimes the most ordinary-looking hand contains a subtle point. I will make this problem a little easier by indicating the moment at which the critical play occurred.

North
♠ 10 8 4
♡ 8 4 2
♢ 9 6 4
♣ Q J 9 3

East
♠ K 6 3
♡ A K 9 5
♢ 10 7 3
♣ K 8 4

North was the dealer with neither side vulnerable. This was the bidding:

South	West	North	East
—	—	No	1NT
dble	No	2♣	No
3♠	No	4♠	No
No	No		

North's raise to four spades was—well, imaginative. West began with the queen of hearts and followed with the jack. East overtook and South followed. What should East play now?

Thinking that it could hardly matter, East led a third heart.

When you look at the full diagram you will see why this was a mistake.

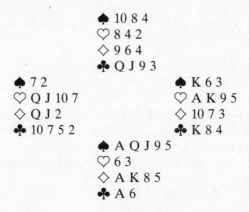

```
                    ♠ 10 8 4
                    ♡ 8 4 2
                    ◇ 9 6 4
                    ♣ Q J 9 3
    ♠ 7 2                         ♠ K 6 3
    ♡ Q J 10 7                    ♡ A K 9 5
    ◇ Q J 2                       ◇ 10 7 3
    ♣ 10 7 5 2                    ♣ K 8 4
                    ♠ A Q J 9 5
                    ♡ 6 3
                    ◇ A K 8 5
                    ♣ A 6
```

South ruffed the third heart and played off ace, king and another diamond. What could West do now? A fourth heart is as good as anything. South ruffs with dummy's 8 of spades, leads the queen of clubs, and successfully picks up both black kings.

It wasn't easy, perhaps, but East should have been careful to leave his side with an off-play card. After the second heart he must play a diamond. Now if South follows the same line as before, the defenders have a safe card of exit.

POINTS TO REMEMBER

1. I described North's raise to four spades as imaginative, but that was not a criticism. To hold three trumps in this type of auction is an important asset. South might have had a six-card suit, but it would still have been dangerous for him to bid game on his own.

2. East should have seen at once that it might be vital not to give dummy an entry for finesses in the black suits. The best play, probably, is to overtake the first heart and switch to a diamond.

10 Tactical Error

What would you open on the North hand below? In the trials for the 1981 European Championship I played with Colin Simpson, a very talented player who is sure to play at international level before long. You may think that I let him down on this deal.

```
              ♠ J 9 8 7
              ♡ K 2
              ♢ A J 10 9 8 7 6
              ♣ —
♣ 6 led
              ♠ A 10 6
              ♡ A Q 4
              ♢ K 5 2
              ♣ 8 5 4 3
```

North was the dealer and we were vulnerable. I opened one diamond, which I think is right, East passed, and South responded 3NT. That, perhaps, is typical of a rubber bridge rather than a tournament player. I had a tricky decision now. At pairs it would be right to pass, since once you leave 3NT behind you are more or less committed to playing in a slam, five of a minor being too narrow a target. At I.M.P. the primary objective is to score a game and I think that in the present circumstances, at any rate, I was wrong to pass. Certainly it seemed so when West led the 6 of clubs and East's 10 held the first trick.

The continuation was rather strange. After the 10 of clubs East led the king, followed by the queen, then switched to the king of spades. Suddenly back in the game, South won with the ace and

40

laid down the king of diamonds. But alas, West showed out and the contract was now in ruins. This was the full hand:

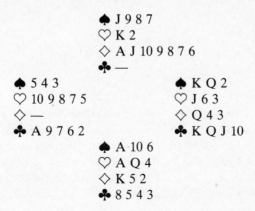

♠ J 9 8 7
♡ K 2
♢ A J 10 9 8 7 6
♣ —

♠ 5 4 3
♡ 10 9 8 7 5
♢ —
♣ A 9 7 6 2

♠ K Q 2
♡ J 6 3
♢ Q 4 3
♣ K Q J 10

♠ A 10 6
♡ A Q 4
♢ K 5 2
♣ 8 5 4 3

It wasn't really difficult to work out why East, with five club tricks in the bag, had switched to the king of spades. He must have thought he had a trick in diamonds. As he was the first to say, Colin could have turned the tables by crossing to the ace of diamonds and running the jack if West showed out.

East was pleased with the result, but obviously he could have ensured his trick in spades by the safer play of continuing clubs and discarding his lowest heart on the fifth club.

POINTS TO REMEMBER

1. A response of 3NT to an opening bid of one is common in pairs and at rubber bridge, but in team play most good players use the response only on flat hands with a guard in all the unbid suits. Otherwise, it is difficult for the opener to know what to do when he is unbalanced.

2. When a defender makes an unexpected play, always try to work out what is going through his mind. It is generally quite easy to find the answer.

11 Tale of Two Kings

In Terence Reese's book *The Expert Game* there is a chapter entitled 'Hold It!' which impressed me when I was learning the game. One of the points he made was that when the declarer was developing a two-suited hand a defender should be reluctant to part with a control in the main side suit. An example occurred on this deal from a match at the Acol club:

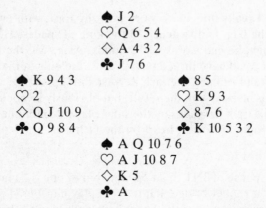

At both tables South played in six hearts and West led the queen of diamonds. The play by declarer is not so easy as it may seem. If he wins in dummy and leads the queen of hearts he may, for all he knows, be unable to return to dummy for the spade finesse. Apparently needing just one of two finesses, both declarers formed the plan of winning with the ace of diamonds and leading a low spade to the queen. If this loses, then the jack of spades will be an entry for the trump finesse.

This plan worked at one table, but at the other I did not part with the king of spades when South led low to the queen. I knew from experience that such tricks usually come back. When the queen of spades held, the position was:

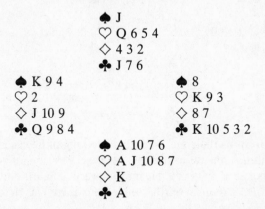

♠ J
♥ Q 6 5 4
♦ 4 3 2
♣ J 7 6

♠ K 9 4
♥ 2
♦ J 10 9
♣ Q 9 8 4

♠ 8
♥ K 9 3
♦ 8 7
♣ K 10 5 3 2

♠ A 10 7 6
♥ A J 10 8 7
♦ K
♣ A

South followed with the ace of spades and a third round which he incautiously ruffed low. East overruffed with the nine and South, with no entry to the table, was obliged to lose another trick.

Naturally North pointed out that South could have afforded to ruff the third spade with the queen of hearts. This also leads to an interesting possibility. Suppose that South cashes ace of spades and ruffs the next round with the queen. East does *not* overruff, so this is the situation:

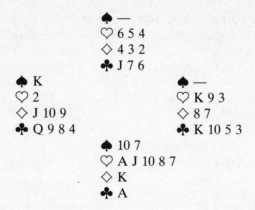

♠ —
♡ 6 5 4
♢ 4 3 2
♣ J 7 6

♠ K
♡ 2
♢ J 10 9
♣ Q 9 8 4

♠ —
♡ K 9 3
♢ 8 7
♣ K 10 5 3

♠ 10 7
♡ A J 10 8 7
♢ K
♣ A

If South forms the conclusion that the king of hearts is on his left he will not finesse in trumps, because West might win and give partner a ruff with ♡9. He may play ace of hearts and follow with the jack; then a third round from East will defeat the contract.

POINTS TO REMEMBER

1. It is almost always good play to hold up a control in the declarer's second suit. For example, if declarer leads a singleton from dummy and, sitting over his long side suit, you hold A x x x, it is almost always right to hold up the ace.

2. Also, as most players know, it is often good play to refuse to overruff. In the second sequence described above, East can see that he will not lose his trump trick. It is more daring to refuse to overruff with holdings such as A x or K x, but this play too will often work well, because declarer will form a wrong conclusion.

12 A Question of Balance

I wonder if you will see how declarer's play on this deal from match play could have been improved.

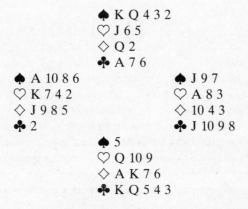

♠ K Q 4 3 2
♡ J 6 5
◇ Q 2
♣ A 7 6

♠ A 10 8 6　　　　♠ J 9 7
♡ K 7 4 2　　　　♡ A 8 3
◇ J 9 8 5　　　　◇ 10 4 3
♣ 2　　　　♣ J 10 9 8

♠ 5
♡ Q 10 9
◇ A K 7 6
♣ K Q 5 4 3

The contract at both tables was the natural 3NT. At one table West—rather foolishly in my opinion—began with the deceptive lead of ♠8 through dummy's suit. It wasn't difficult now for South to make four tricks in clubs, three in diamonds, and one in each of the majors (or two in spades).

At the other table West led a heart to the ace and ducked the heart return. In with ♡10, South played ace and king of clubs, to find that the suit was not breaking. As he could not afford to lose three hearts, a spade and a club, South followed with a spade to the king. The position now was:

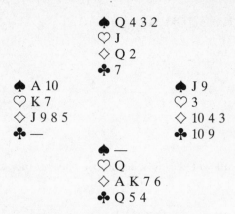

```
              ♠ Q 4 3 2
              ♡ J
              ◇ Q 2
              ♣ 7
♠ A 10                      ♠ J 9
♡ K 7                       ♡ 3
◇ J 9 8 5                   ◇ 10 4 3
♣ —                         ♣ 10 9
              ♠ —
              ♡ Q
              ◇ A K 7 6
              ♣ Q 5 4
```

The declarer gave long consideration to his next play, but was unable to find a good answer. Whatever he does now, the result will be the same.

'I'm sure I ought to have made it somehow,' South lamented.

There was indeed a way, not at all easy to see in time. When in with the heart at trick two, South should reflect on these lines:

'No problem if the clubs break. What is going to happen if they don't? The only chance I can see is that two discards may be difficult for a player who holds ace of spades, the long hearts, and four diamonds. If this is the situation I mustn't lose contact with the dummy, because in that case the spades will no longer be a threat.'

So the right play is to start off with king and queen of clubs from hand. On the second club West's only safe discard is a spade. The position is then:

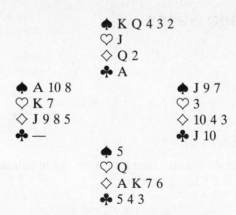

```
            ♠ K Q 4 3 2
            ♡ J
            ◇ Q 2
            ♣ A
♠ A 10 8                      ♠ J 9 7
♡ K 7                         ♡ 3
◇ J 9 8 5                     ◇ 10 4 3
♣ —                          ♣ J 10
            ♠ 5
            ♡ Q
            ◇ A K 7 6
            ♣ 5 4 3
```

South leads a spade to the king, on which West must play low, and follows with the ace of clubs. Now West is *kaput*! He cannot throw a diamond, obviously; if he bares the ace of spades he will be thrown in with a low spade; and if he lets go a winning heart he can be thrown in later and forced to give dummy another trick in spades.

POINTS TO REMEMBER

1. There is a type of player who will always favour a deceptive lead such as a middle card from A 10 x x through dummy's suit. Such leads gain on occasions, but here West had length in the only unbid suit and sufficient entries to make a heart lead promising.

2. Since the contract was going to be lay-down if the clubs were breaking, South had to consider the possibility that they might not. The advantage of beginning with king and queen of clubs, rather than ace and another, was that declarer could maintain a better entry-balance. The fact that he was in dummy after the third round of clubs enabled him to exert pressure in spades as well as the other suits.

13   Second String

This exciting deal came up in the 1981 trials to find Britain's team for the European Championship:

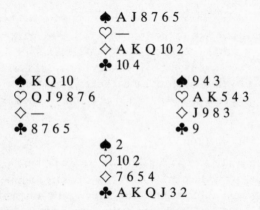

```
                    ♠ A J 8 7 6 5
                    ♡ —
                    ◇ A K Q 10 2
                    ♣ 10 4
♠ K Q 10                          ♠ 9 4 3
♡ Q J 9 8 7 6                     ♡ A K 5 4 3
◇ —                               ◇ J 9 8 3
♣ 8 7 6 5                         ♣ 9
                    ♠ 2
                    ♡ 10 2
                    ◇ 7 6 5 4
                    ♣ A K Q J 3 2
```

Some East-West pairs defended in six hearts against six clubs or six diamonds. I held the West cards and my partner and I decided to take our chance against six clubs after this bidding:

South	West	North	East
—	No	1♠	No
2♣	2♡	3◇	4♡
5♣	5♡	6♣	No
No	No		

Opponents were vulnerable, but with my void in diamonds I had the feeling that we might have chances in defence.

48

The heart lead was ruffed in dummy and the 10 of clubs was cashed. South entered his hand with ace of spades and a spade ruff and drew trumps, discarding three spades from dummy. This left:

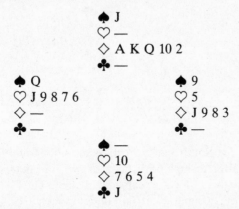

```
              ♠ J
              ♡ —
              ◇ A K Q 10 2
              ♣ —
♠ Q                        ♠ 9
♡ J 9 8 7 6                ♡ 5
◇ —                        ◇ J 9 8 3
♣ —                        ♣ —
              ♠ —
              ♡ 10
              ◇ 7 6 5 4
              ♣ J
```

A diamond to dummy brought the bitter news that the suit was not breaking, so South was one down, losing a diamond and a heart.

Nothing was said and I don't know to this day whether the opponents realized that the contract should have been made. South could have given himself an additional chance. Look again at the declarer's position after the second round of trumps:

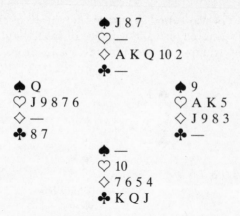

♠ J 8 7
♡ —
♢ A K Q 10 2
♣ —

♠ Q   ♠ 9
♡ J 9 8 7 6   ♡ A K 5
♢ —   ♢ J 9 8 3
♣ 8 7   ♣ —

♠ —
♡ 10
♢ 7 6 5 4
♣ K Q J

At this point South can afford to discard *diamonds* from dummy. If, after trumps have been drawn, the diamonds are seen to be breaking, declarer can come back to hand with a ruff to make the fourth diamond; if diamonds are seen to be 4–0 there is still time to play for a 3–3 break in spades.

POINTS TO REMEMBER

1. I might have been wrong here not to sacrifice over six clubs, but from experience I believe that slam sacrifices in any multi-table event are overdone. Quite often one loses 700, which *should* be a good result, only to find that the slam has not been bid at some tables or that opponents have doubled too soon and have taken only 500.

2. When dummy has two long side suits, try always to organize the play so that a favourable break in either suit will win the contract.

14   She Knows, y'Know

It is always annoying to let a game slip through when your side could have taken the first four tricks. East–West on this deal were a mixed partnership. North was the dealer at game all and these were the hands of North and East:

```
        ♠ A K 10 5
        ♡ J 2
        ◇ Q 9 6 4
        ♣ Q 8 7
                    ♠ 3 2
                    ♡ A 9 3
        ♡ 8 led     ◇ A K 8 7
                    ♣ K 9 6 4
```

The bidding went:

South	West	North	East
—	—	1◇	No
1♠	No	2♠	No
4♠	No	No	No

East won the lead of ♡8 with the ace, South playing low. On the king of diamonds South dropped the jack and West the 3. First question: what should East play next?

It is possible, though not very likely, that partner has a doubleton 3 2. More likely, he has played the 3 from 10 5 3 2 or from 10 5 3. Deciding in the end that she was unlikely to beat the contract unless her partner held the ace of clubs, East laid down the king of clubs; jack from declarer, 5 from partner. After studying this card for a while, East led another club. Disaster, for the full hand was:

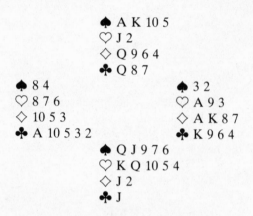

```
            ♠ A K 10 5
            ♡ J 2
            ◇ Q 9 6 4
            ♣ Q 8 7
♠ 8 4                      ♠ 3 2
♡ 8 7 6                    ♡ A 9 3
◇ 10 5 3                   ◇ A K 8 7
♣ A 10 5 3 2              ♣ K 9 6 4
            ♠ Q J 9 7 6
            ♡ K Q 10 5 4
            ◇ J 2
            ♣ J
```

South ruffed the second club and after drawing trumps was able to discard three diamonds from the dummy.

What was the mistake in the defence? West tried to blame his partner, but I think he was wrong to play the 5 of clubs. West knows that partner knows that he, West, holds the ace of clubs. It was correct, therefore, to signal the *count*. If West had played the 2 of clubs—lowest from an odd number—East would have been able to work out the right continuation.

POINTS TO REMEMBER

1. East missed one clue. With 10532 of diamonds West would, or certainly should, have given a clearer signal by dropping the 5, not the 3.

2. Sometimes a defender wants to tell partner about high cards, sometimes about the count. To my mind, the right system to follow is this: show encouragement or discouragement when it is important to show partner that you hold, or do not hold, strength; when partner can work this out for himself, indicate length. The usual method is to play the lowest card from an odd number, high-low from an even number.

15 By Any Other Name

In my first book I described a hand where declarer leads a side suit and ruffs, to the embarrassment of a defender who is forced to make what in the end turns out to be a fatal discard. Is this a squeeze? I wouldn't care to say, but certainly it is one of the most attractive and least understood forms of play.

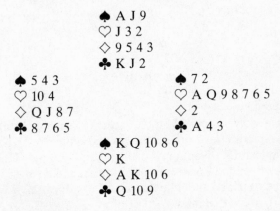

```
                    ♠ A J 9
                    ♡ J 3 2
                    ♢ 9 5 4 3
                    ♣ K J 2
    ♠ 5 4 3                        ♠ 7 2
    ♡ 10 4                         ♡ A Q 9 8 7 6 5
    ♢ Q J 8 7                      ♢ 2
    ♣ 8 7 6 5                      ♣ A 4 3
                    ♠ K Q 10 8 6
                    ♡ K
                    ♢ A K 10 6
                    ♣ Q 10 9
```

I held the South cards at rubber bridge and we were vulnerable. The bidding went:

South	West	North	East
1♠	No	2♠	4♡
4♠	No	No	No

East won the first trick with the ace of hearts and shifted promptly to the 2 of diamonds. I won with the ace and took stock. If the 2 of diamonds was a singleton, which seemed likely, I would be able to end-play West if he held, say, 4–2–4–3

53

distribution, but not if he held four clubs and discarded correctly. At this stage it seemed fairly safe to test the clubs, so I led the 10 of clubs. East won the second round and returned a club, confirming my suspicion that the diamonds were 4–1.

I led a spade to the jack, ruffed a heart, and led a second spade to the ace. The position then was:

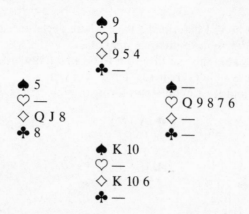

♠ 9
♡ J
♢ 9 5 4
♣ —

♠ 5   ♠ —
♡ —   ♡ Q 9 8 7 6
♢ Q J 8   ♢ —
♣ 8   ♣ —

♠ K 10
♡ —
♢ K 10 6
♣ —

If I draw the trump I lose the contract. Instead, I ruffed the third heart with the 10 of spades. Now consider West's position. If he underruffs I lead a low diamond and end-play him; if he throws a diamond I play king and another, and he must give me the last two tricks; and if he throws a club I draw the trump and exit with a low diamond.

POINTS TO REMEMBER

1. Most players would have lost their chance on this hand by drawing trumps early on. There was no risk in playing on clubs, and this helped declarer to build up a picture of the hand.

2. Considering how much is written about squeeze play, it is strange that endings of this type are so seldom described. It is often good play to take a ruff in a suit of which one opponent is void. Whereas at chess it is usually good play to *force* an opponent's move, at bridge it often helps to make the opponent choose.

16   On the Wild Side

What would you expect the contract to be on this deal from match play? North was the dealer and East–West were vulnerable.

```
              ♠ 3 2
              ♡ K Q 8 7 5
              ◇ K J 7 6 5
              ♣ 2
♠ 8 6                      ♠ A K Q J 10 9 7
♡ 9 6 4 3                  ♡ 10
◇ 9 8 3                    ◇ Q 10 2
♣ J 9 5 4                  ♣ K Q
              ♠ 5 4
              ♡ A J 2
              ◇ A 4
              ♣ A 10 8 7 6 3
```

Well, I dare say you guessed, because I usually make South the declarer. I was East and the bidding went like this:

South	West	North	East
—	—	No	4♠
No	No	4NT(!)	dble
5♣	No	5◇	dble
5♡	No	No	dble
No	No	No	

North's 4NT was on the wild side, but he found a good hand opposite.

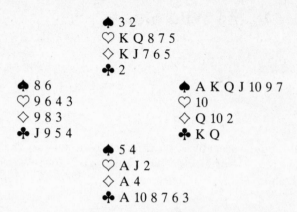

♠ 3 2
♡ K Q 8 7 5
♢ K J 7 6 5
♣ 2

♠ 8 6
♡ 9 6 4 3
♢ 9 8 3
♣ J 9 5 4

♠ A K Q J 10 9 7
♡ 10
♢ Q 10 2
♣ K Q

♠ 5 4
♡ A J 2
♢ A 4
♣ A 10 8 7 6 3

West led ♠8 and I cashed two spade tricks. What next? Well, it wasn't difficult to judge that South must hold three aces and that he could not hold as many as three diamonds. So I thought it could do no harm to play a third round of spades.

Would you expect South to make the contract now? He played well. Discarding a club from hand, he ruffed in dummy. West, meanwhile, threw a diamond, so after ace and king of diamonds the position was:

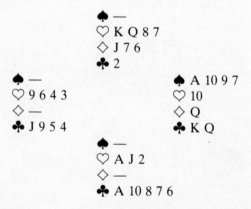

♠ —
♡ K Q 8 7
♢ J 7 6
♣ 2

♠ —
♡ 9 6 4 3
♢ —
♣ J 9 5 4

♠ A 10 9 7
♡ 10
♢ Q
♣ K Q

♠ —
♡ A J 2
♢ —
♣ A 10 8 7 6

South ruffed the next diamond with the jack of hearts, cashed the ace, and after due reflection finessed the 8 of hearts to land the contract.

56

At the other table North opened with a flighty one heart, East bid four spades, and South five hearts, which was passed out. East cashed two spades and followed with the king of clubs. When East showed out on the second heart North followed with ace and another diamond. Fortunately for my side he went up with the king now and so made the contract, but we still lost 5 match points.

POINTS TO REMEMBER

1. Some players—the type who answer bidding problems in magazines—would say that East was too strong to open four spades. All good players make this sort of bid at rubber bridge and I am sure it is not wrong at any form of scoring. Just occasionally you may miss a slam, but there is plenty of compensation.

2. When you can see that the declarer has no loser he can usefully discard, don't hesitate to give him a ruff and discard. This play is all the more effective when partner is able to discard as well.

17   Two Ways to Kill

When the following hand was played at rubber bridge I was
sitting behind East. It seemed to me that the defence was pretty
obvious. See if you agree.

```
              ♠ Q J 2
              ♡ Q 10 7
              ◇ 3 2
              ♣ K 9 8 7 6
                          ♠ A 3
                          ♡ A K J 4
   ♡ 5 led                ◇ 9 8 6 5
                          ♣ Q 10 4
```

East opened one heart at game all and the bidding continued:

South	West	North	East
—	—	—	1♡
2♣	4♡	4♠	No
No	No		

West led a low heart, East won with the jack, and South
followed. East made the natural switch to a diamond, on which
South played the queen and West the king. West returned the
jack of diamonds to the declarer's ace. A low spade went to the
jack and ace. What should East play now?

The player I was watching made the 'easy' play of a high heart.
If you look at the full hand you will soon see why this was wrong.

58

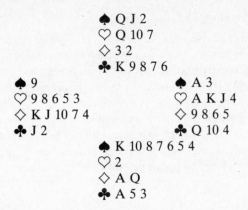

The play has gone: heart to jack, diamond to queen and king, diamond to ace, spade to jack and ace. When East led a high heart South ruffed and played trumps, arriving at this position:

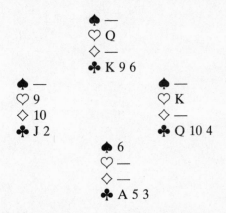

A club was thrown from dummy on the last trump and East was squeezed.

Was this difficult to foresee? I don't think so. In any case, to lead earlier from ♣ Q 10 x could hardly cost; the play would be more difficult (but still correct) from Q J x.

1. A high proportion of contracts made by squeeze play could be defeated by better defence. One possibility here was to kill the menace in hearts by playing this suit three times. After the king of diamonds West could have led a second heart, and East a third heart when he won with the ace of spades.

2. The second way to beat the squeeze was to destroy the necessary communications. When in with the ace of spades East could see that dummy held a menace card in hearts and it was essential, therefore, to break up the communication in clubs.

18   Definitely No Overtrick

One of the pleasures of a big pairs tournament is to compare scores with a friend who has played the same way as yourself. 'We had one horrible board,' my friend remarked at the beginning. We soon came to it.

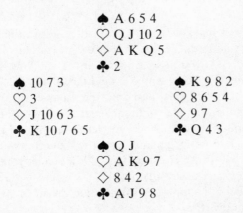

```
              ♠ A 6 5 4
              ♡ Q J 10 2
              ◇ A K Q 5
              ♣ 2
♠ 10 7 3                      ♠ K 9 8 2
♡ 3                           ♡ 8 6 5 4
◇ J 10 6 3                    ◇ 9 7
♣ K 10 7 6 5                  ♣ Q 4 3
              ♠ Q J
              ♡ A K 9 7
              ◇ 8 4 2
              ♣ A J 9 8
```

'Plus 1430,' I said, reading from our scoresheet.

'That was our bad one. Minus 100.'

'Why, did you play in 6NT or something?'

'No, I opened 1NT and we finished in six hearts, like most people, I imagine. What lead did you get?'

'A club, I think. My partner played it. He didn't seem to find any problem. He lost the spade finesse, discarded a diamond on the ace of spades, and crossruffed.'

'Ah, well, I got a heart lead. Nobody had told West about

leading singleton trumps. I won with the 7 and finessed the spade at once. East returned a heart. Now look at the position:

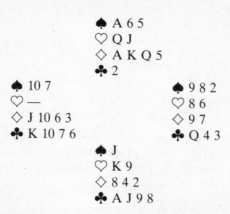

♠ A 6 5
♡ Q J
◇ A K Q 5
♣ 2

♠ 10 7
♡ —
◇ J 10 6 3
♣ K 10 7 6

♠ 9 8 2
♡ 8 6
◇ 9 7
♣ Q 4 3

♠ J
♡ K 9
◇ 8 4 2
♣ A J 9 8

'The obvious line is to take a club ruff, return to the jack of spades, and ruff another club. I can throw my last club on the ace of spades, but now I'm in dummy and I can't do it unless diamonds are 3–3. So instead I cashed the jack of spades, took one club ruff, cashed ♠A, and drew the trumps. But West held on to his diamonds and I couldn't make it. Do you see any way?'

'No, I don't think you can do it from this position,' I replied. 'Let's go back to the beginning. Suppose that after winning the trump lead you ruff a club and lead a low spade from dummy towards the Q J. Doesn't that do it?'

'Well . . . yes. I suppose so. But I didn't want to give up the chance of an overtrick.'

POINTS TO REMEMBER

1. There is a popular theory that it is wrong to lead a singleton trump because of the danger of killing partner's possible Q x x. But the lead is sound enough when it looks as though the trumps are 4–4–4–1 round the table. Partner may win an early trick and be able to lead a second round with good effect.

2. With Q J opposite A x x x you are only going to make two tricks, so on many hands the finesse is an illusion. It is true that on

this deal South would have had chances of making seven if the spade finesse had been right and the diamonds 3–3. However, in a big pairs event it is foolish to risk failing in a good slam contract which some pairs won't reach.

19   Early Test

Sometimes you start off with a poor hand, the opponents reach a game contract, and you think you won't have anything to do. A critical play is necessary early on, and if you are not awake you won't realize you have anything to do.

```
              ♠ 4 2
              ♡ A 10 8
              ◇ A 9 6 2
              ♣ A K 9 3
                            ♠ 9 8 7
                            ♡ 6 2
    ♠ K led                 ◇ J 7 5 3
                            ♣ Q J 6 2
```

You are East, your side is vulnerable, and the bidding goes:

South	West	North	East
—	1 ♠	dble	No
4 ♡	No	No	No

Partner opens with king and ace of spades, South dropping the queen on the second round. Partner shifts to a low heart, which is won in dummy, South plays a diamond to the king, on which West plays the 8, and takes two more rounds of trumps. Partner follows suit and on the third round you discard your third spade.

The declarer leads ◇ A from the table and . . . but you've already made the fatal play!

Why was it wrong to discard your third spade? Look at the full deal:

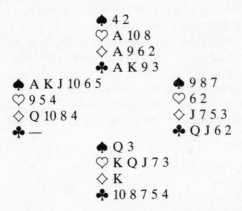

```
                    ♠ 4 2
                    ♡ A 10 8
                    ◇ A 9 6 2
                    ♣ A K 9 3
    ♠ A K J 10 6 5              ♠ 9 8 7
    ♡ 9 5 4                     ♡ 6 2
    ◇ Q 10 8 4                  ◇ J 7 5 3
    ♣ —                         ♣ Q J 6 2
                    ♠ Q 3
                    ♡ K Q J 7 3
                    ◇ K
                    ♣ 10 8 7 5 4
```

Remember how the play has gone: two top spades, a trump to the 8, a diamond to the king, two more trumps, and you have discarded your third spade. The play is quite easy for South now. He plays ace of diamonds and ruffs a diamond, crosses to the king of clubs and ruffs the fourth diamond. You are down to ♣ Q J 6 and are end-played when a club is ducked to the jack.

Was it difficult to foresee this? Not really. You have seen declarer play the king of diamonds, so he surely has nine tricks on top—five hearts and four top winners in the minor suits. What is the diamond situation? Partner dropped the 8, remember, when South led a diamond to the king. You must place West with the queen of diamonds to have any chance, and if he has Q 8 alone you will not be able to prevent South from establishing a long diamond. In any case, why has declarer played a diamond to the king early on? Surely because he has a singleton king and is clearing the decks in case he needs to eliminate diamonds. If West has ◇ Q 10 8 4 you must not allow the declarer to end-play you in clubs: you must keep your third spade and discard a diamond now.

1. Players tend to think that such cards as East's third spade are useless and dispensable. That is wrong. Always keep in mind that you may later need a safe card of exit.

2. South's early play of a diamond to the king was a sure indication that he had a singleton and was preparing for ruffs. When such a play is made, don't just follow suit—ask yourself what is happening and don't play to the next trick until you have worked out the answer. Note, also, that it was very good play by the declarer to prepare for the possibility of the clubs being 4–0.

20 Those 5–4 Hands

A tricky defensive problem arose on this deal, which few players would solve in a logical way. I will begin by showing only the West and North cards.

                    ♠ Q 10 7 5
                    ♡ K 10 9 4
                    ◇ Q J
                    ♣ 8 4 2
    ♠ K 8 3
    ♡ 7
    ◇ 10 6 5 2
    ♣ Q 9 7 5 3

The bidding went:

South	West	North	East
1♡	No	2♡	No
2♠	No	3♠	No
4♠	No	No	No

It is normally not good play to lead a singleton into the declarer's side suit, but holding a trick in spades West began with his singleton heart. South won in hand with the 8 and played ace and another spade. Hoping for a ruff, West went up with the king and his partner followed suit. The problem now was whether to switch to a diamond or a club. Three more tricks are needed, remember. See if you can arrive at a logical answer.

Take the possibilities in turn. If partner has neither of the minor suit aces, it won't matter what you do now. If he has king of diamonds and ace of clubs you can take a club trick and a heart ruff, but this will be all. To make *three* more tricks you need to find partner with ace of diamonds and king of clubs, so it is right to switch to a diamond. The full hand was:

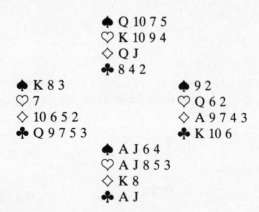

♠ Q 10 7 5
♡ K 10 9 4
♢ Q J
♣ 8 4 2

♠ K 8 3
♡ 7
♢ 10 6 5 2
♣ Q 9 7 5 3

♠ 9 2
♡ Q 6 2
♢ A 9 7 4 3
♣ K 10 6

♠ A J 6 4
♡ A J 8 5 3
♢ K 8
♣ A J

At the table West tried a club when in with the king of spades. It was easy then for South to draw the outstanding trump and concede just three tricks.

POINTS TO REMEMBER

1. Having been supported in both suits, South had to decide whether to try for game in hearts, probably 5–4, or in spades, doubtless 4–4. To play in the 4–4 suit tends to be better when the declarer is 5–4–2–2, because the discard on the five-card suit may be valuable. When a player with 5–4–3–1 shape knows that his partner can support both suits, there is usually no advantage in playing in the 4–4 suit.

2. There was a reasonable case here for the lead of a singleton in the declarer's side suit, and, as we have seen, the contract could have been defeated. But if West had led one of the minor suits South would probably have misguessed the hearts and been one down. The lead of a singleton in declarer's side suit is sometimes worth considering against a slam contract, but for the rest I avoid it. Too often it kills a holding such as K J x or K 10 x x in partner's hand.

21 Long May They Continue

Some tournament players announce that their overcalls at the one level, when not vulnerable, are simply a 'noise'. What a silly idea this is! By entering the auction with very little strength they simply tell the eventual declarer about their distribution. It is true that to overcall one club with one spade deprives the opponents of bidding space, and there are some grounds for doing this on minimum values. But I can see no sense in overcalling one heart with one spade on the sort of values that West held on this deal from a pairs tournament at Crans:

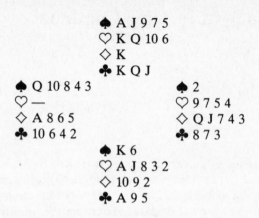

```
                    ♠ A J 9 7 5
                    ♡ K Q 10 6
                    ◇ K
                    ♣ K Q J
♠ Q 10 8 4 3                        ♠ 2
♡ —                                 ♡ 9 7 5 4
◇ A 8 6 5                           ◇ Q J 7 4 3
♣ 10 6 4 2                          ♣ 8 7 3
                    ♠ K 6
                    ♡ A J 8 3 2
                    ◇ 10 9 2
                    ♣ A 9 5
```

North–South were vulnerable and the bidding went like this:

South	West	North	East
1♡	1♠	2♠	No
2NT	No	3♡	No
4♡	No	4NT	No
5◇	No	6♡	No
No	No		

After some shuffling from suit to suit, West led a low spade. I could have won this trick with the 6, but since West was marked with length and the suit was probably divided 5–1, I thought that my position would be more flexible if I won with the king.

A round of trumps brought the news that the hearts were 4–0. This was something of a shock, because I had expected to be able to draw trumps, ruff one diamond and, if necessary, finesse in spades to obtain a discard for the third diamond. As it was, I could not force out the ace of diamonds before I had drawn all the trumps. After the trumps I took three rounds of clubs, arriving at the position opposite:

On the last heart West threw a diamond and dummy a spade. A finesse of ♠ 9, followed by a diamond exit, provided a pretty ending.

70

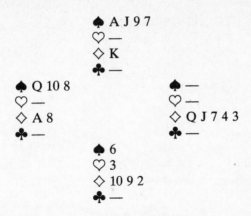

♠ A J 9 7
♡ —
◇ K
♣ —

♠ Q 10 8
♡ —
◇ A 8
♣ —

♠ —
♡ —
◇ Q J 7 4 3
♣ —

♠ 6
♡ 3
◇ 10 9 2
♣ —

At some tables where spades had not been mentioned a club was led against six hearts. South can make the contract now if he draws just one trump, gives up a diamond, and ruffs two more diamonds with high trumps; but some declarers led a diamond before drawing a round of trumps, won the next club with the ace, and ruffed a diamond with ♡ 6. After a spade to the king and another diamond ruff they tried to cash the ace of spades and ran into a ruff. This emphasizes the folly of making a sub-minimum overcall and warning the declarer of the spade situation.

POINTS TO REMEMBER

1. The weaker side gains *nothing* by entering the auction on poor hands. The more unusual the distribution, the more it pays to conceal this fact. With a hand such as West held here the sensible action is to pass on the first round and contest later if the bidding by the opposition sounds weak.

2. Looking at the deal again, I see that if I had won the first trick with the 6 of spades I could still have end-played West by playing off all the trumps, cashing ♠ K, and crossing to dummy on the third round of clubs. However, it is better play in general to keep the entries fluid.

22 A Little Knowledge

'Do you think I ought to have made this contract?' asked a friend, showing me this deal:

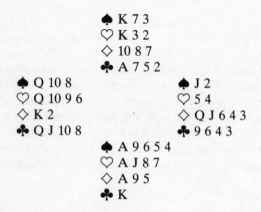

```
              ♠ K 7 3
              ♡ K 3 2
              ◇ 10 8 7
              ♣ A 7 5 2
♠ Q 10 8                    ♠ J 2
♡ Q 10 9 6                  ♡ 5 4
◇ K 2                       ◇ Q J 6 4 3
♣ Q J 10 8                  ♣ 9 6 4 3
              ♠ A 9 6 5 4
              ♡ A J 8 7
              ◇ A 9 5
              ♣ K
```

The bidding went:

South	West	North	East
1 ♠	No	2 ♣	No
2 ♡	No	3 ♠	No
4 ♠	No	No	No

'I won the club lead,' South explained, 'drew two rounds of trumps, and discarded a diamond on the the ace of clubs. Then I played ace, king and a low heart. That's the right safety play, isn't it? But you see the position now:

72

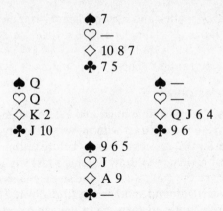

♠ 7
♡ —
◇ 10 8 7
♣ 7 5

♠ Q   ♠ —
♡ Q   ♡ —
◇ K 2   ◇ Q J 6 4
♣ J 10   ♣ 9 6

♠ 9 6 5
♡ J
◇ A 9
♣ —

'West drew the trump and made a heart and a diamond for one down. My partner didn't say anything, but I have an idea he wasn't pleased.'

'You certainly weren't lucky,' I said carefully. 'But I'm not sure it was right to draw the top trumps early on. What killed you was West being able to extract the last trump from dummy. Suppose you win the opening club lead, cross to the king of spades and finesse the jack of hearts, losing to the queen. This is the position:

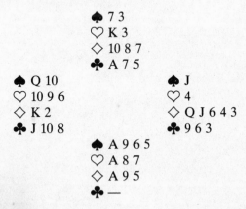

♠ 7 3
♡ K 3
◇ 10 8 7
♣ A 7 5

♠ Q 10   ♠ J
♡ 10 9 6   ♡ 4
◇ K 2   ◇ Q J 6 4 3
♣ J 10 8   ♣ 9 6 3

♠ A 9 6 5
♡ A 8 7
◇ A 9 5
♣ —

'Say that West exits with a club to dummy's ace. You draw a

second round of spades and play on hearts, ruffing the fourth round. That looks all right. You lose a spade, a heart and a diamond.'

'I suppose you're right. These safety plays are overrated.'

POINTS TO REMEMBER

1. This was a fairly simple hand and I dare say most players would have made the contract without any difficulty. The basic error was to draw two rounds of trumps before testing the hearts, so giving West a chance to draw dummy's last trump.

2. But perhaps the hand wasn't quite so easy, because a pupil to whom I showed it found another way to go down. He took just one round of trumps and then made the same sort of play in hearts—ace, king and a third round. Now West played a fourth round and East made a trick with the jack of spades. Of course, to play ace, king and a low heart is indeed the best way to make three tricks with this combination, considered on its own, but the whole idea was foolish here because the fourth heart would not provide a useful discard of any kind. Meanwhile, there was the threat of losing an extra trick in the trump suit.

23   Won by an Inch

I suppose the reason why I like pairs better than any other form of the game is that if I can make one more trick than most of the others in a popular contract this trick will be worth a fair number of match points. To make 450 instead of 420 in match play will win you just one I.M.P., but in a pairs it may make the difference between an average and a shared top. This hand was played in one of the big events at the Europa Hotel in London.

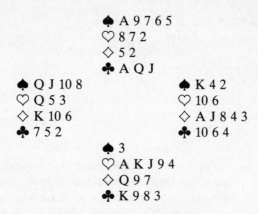

```
                    ♠ A 9 7 6 5
                    ♡ 8 7 2
                    ◇ 5 2
                    ♣ A Q J
    ♠ Q J 10 8                 ♠ K 4 2
    ♡ Q 5 3                    ♡ 10 6
    ◇ K 10 6                   ◇ A J 8 4 3
    ♣ 7 5 2                    ♣ 10 6 4
                    ♠ 3
                    ♡ A K J 9 4
                    ◇ Q 9 7
                    ♣ K 9 8 3
```

Like almost everyone else, I imagine, my partner and I
finished in four hearts after this bidding:

South	North
1♡	1♠
2♣	2◇
2♡	4♡
No	

North bid the fourth suit, two diamonds, to see if I could rebid
my hearts.

West led a spade, won by the ace in dummy. In a team game it
would probably be right to lead a diamond now, preparing for a
diamond ruff, but in a pairs I like to give myself additional
chances and at trick two I ruffed a spade. I followed with a low
diamond from hand. East won and shifted to a trump.

I won with the ace of hearts, cashed the king, and led a club to
the jack. I ruffed another spade and made two more club tricks.
This was the position now, with the lead in dummy:

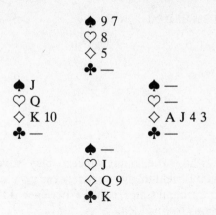

I ruffed a spade and led the king of clubs. What could West do? Whether he ruffs or not, I lose only one more trick and make five.

POINTS TO REMEMBER

1. In match play, or at rubber bridge, the declarer must concentrate on making his contract. In pairs play his objective is to score better than the majority. Thus, if you are in what must be a popular contract, you are justified in taking slight risks for the sake of an extra trick.

2. Though the play was not easy, I think that East should have cashed the second diamond when he was in with ♢8. Since the declarer's diamonds were obviously queen high at best he was marked with the top hearts and the king of clubs. South had bid clubs, so there was really nothing for the defence to take except two diamonds and possibly one heart.

24 Brainwashed

The pundits who write about squeeze play have a habit of declaring that it is right to give up a trick early on to improve the timing for an eventual squeeze. My experience is that there are many exceptions to this idea.

```
              ♠ K J 10
              ♡ 3 2
              ◇ Q 9
              ♣ A Q 10 8 7 6
♠ 7 4 3                        ♠ 9 8 6 5 2
♡ K Q 10 6                     ♡ J 4
◇ J 7 5 4                      ◇ K 6 3 2
♣ 5 2                          ♣ 4 3
              ♠ A Q
              ♡ A 9 8 7 5
              ◇ A 10 8
              ♣ K J 9
```

Six clubs is an easy contract for North–South; depending on the lead, declarer can either make two tricks in diamonds or give up a heart and make the long card a winner. However, this was the final of a tournament in France and most pairs attempted 6NT with an auction along these lines:

South	North
1♡	2♣
3NT	4NT
6NT	No

West leads the king of hearts and South can see eleven tricks on top. Some declarers thought it must be right to duck the opening lead. If West switches to a spade or a club South can succeed by way of a transferred menace (lead ◇ Q, covered by the king, and run the black winners, squeezing West in the red suits). However, if East drops the jack of hearts on the opening lead and West continues with a second heart, South has no play for the contract.

Whether East plays the jack of hearts on the opening lead or not, it is certainly right for South to capture the first trick. He plays off all his black winners, arriving at this sort of position:

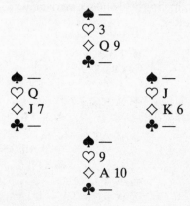

South exits with a heart and at trick 12 West leads a low diamond. South should take the right view now because if West had held ◇ K he would presumably have unblocked in hearts.

POINTS TO REMEMBER

1. As I remarked earlier, 6NT is a favoured contract in a pairs. It scores well if you can make it and sometimes—for example, when the main suit breaks 4–1—you will find that 6NT is easier to make than six of the likely trump suit.

2. Before ducking an early trick 'to rectify the count', be sure you have a picture of the end position you hope to establish. On the present hand, if hearts are led and continued you have almost nothing to play for.

25 Change of Direction

Hands where the natural play is to establish a long suit in dummy often present a problem. South, an international player, lost his contract on the following deal and seemed unaware that he might have played it better.

```
                    ♠ J 3 2
                    ♡ Q J 3
                    ◇ 2
                    ♣ A K J 9 7 2
   ♠ 10 9 7                        ♠ K Q 8 6 5
   ♡ 9 8 5 2                       ♡ 4
   ◇ K J 6 4                       ◇ A 10 9 5
   ♣ 10 3                          ♣ Q 8 6
                    ♠ A 4
                    ♡ A K 10 7 6
                    ◇ Q 8 7 3
                    ♣ 5 4
```

The bidding went:

South	West	North	East
—	—	—	No
1♡	No	2♣	dble
No	2◇	3♡	No
4♡	No	No	No

West led a spade, which ran to the ace. South began by cashing the top clubs and leading a third round from dummy. When East

80

covered, South ruffed high and followed with ace of hearts and a low heart to dummy. This left:

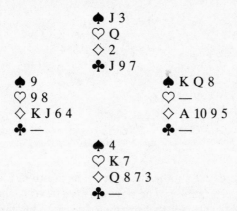

```
                    ♠ J 3
                    ♡ Q
                    ◇ 2
                    ♣ J 9 7
    ♠ 9                             ♠ K Q 8
    ♡ 9 8                           ♡ —
    ◇ K J 6 4                       ◇ A 10 9 5
    ♣ —                             ♣ —
                    ♠ 4
                    ♡ K 7
                    ◇ Q 8 7 3
                    ♣ —
```

Not too well placed now, the declarer led a club from dummy and discarded his spade loser. West ruffed and led a low diamond to his partner's ace. East returned a diamond, forcing dummy to ruff and killing the contract, since West still had to make either a trump and a diamond or two diamonds.

Where did South go wrong? You may not see it at once. Let's go back to the point at which South was in hand after ruffing the third round of clubs.

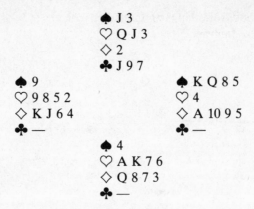

```
                    ♠ J 3
                    ♡ Q J 3
                    ◇ 2
                    ♣ J 9 7
    ♠ 9                          ♠ K Q 8 5
    ♡ 9 8 5 2                    ♡ 4
    ◇ K J 6 4                    ◇ A 10 9 5
    ♣ —                          ♣ —
                    ♠ 4
                    ♡ A K 7 6
                    ◇ Q 8 7 3
                    ♣ —
```

To play ace and another heart now, as South did, is likely to fail if the hearts are 4–1. The right play is a heart to the jack and then the good club, South discarding a spade. This wins whether the trumps are 4–1 or 3–2. West, as the cards lie, ruffs the club, but what can he do next? If he tries to force the dummy by playing diamonds, South can accept the challenge, ruffing a spade in hand, two diamonds in dummy.

POINTS TO REMEMBER

1. This was not a particularly easy hand to play after the spade lead. A finesse of ♣J at trick two may seem a good line, but the defence then is to win with ♣Q, cash a spade, and return a club. On the whole, I don't think the declarer's early play was wrong.

2. As the play went, South should have changed his ideas after East had turned up with three clubs. Since East had doubled North's two clubs after passing originally, it was likely that the hearts would be 4–1. South should have thought about this before playing ace of hearts and a heart to the jack.

26 No Hold-up

My partner said that I made a poor bid on this deal from a team game and perhaps he was right. Still, I did make up for it a little in the play!

$$\spadesuit \text{ A J 7 6 4}$$
$$\heartsuit \text{ 7 5 3}$$
$$\diamondsuit \text{ A J 2}$$
$$\clubsuit \text{ 7 4}$$

♠ 9 2	♠ Q 10 8
♡ 10 8 6 4	♡ J 9
◇ 9 7 5 3	◇ K 10 4
♣ 6 3 2	♣ K Q J 8 5

$$\spadesuit \text{ K 5 3}$$
$$\heartsuit \text{ A K Q 2}$$
$$\diamondsuit \text{ Q 8 6}$$
$$\clubsuit \text{ A 10 9}$$

East was the dealer at game all and the bidding went like this:

South	West	North	East
—	—	—	1♣
dble	No	2♠	No
2NT	No	3NT	No
No	No		

Clearly four spades is a better contract, but my hand was balanced and I couldn't be sure that my partner held a 5-card suit. Incidentally, I regard 2NT as forcing in this sequence; I

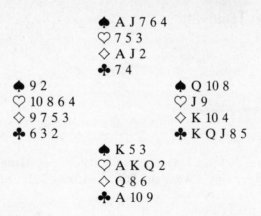

♠ A J 7 6 4
♡ 7 5 3
◇ A J 2
♣ 7 4

♠ 9 2   ♠ Q 10 8
♡ 10 8 6 4   ♡ J 9
◇ 9 7 5 3   ◇ K 10 4
♣ 6 3 2   ♣ K Q J 8 5

♠ K 5 3
♡ A K Q 2
◇ Q 8 6
♣ A 10 9

detest partners who jump in response to a double and fade away on the next round. (If they're going to do that, it's better not to jump in the first place.)

West led the 2 of clubs—best from three small in this situation—and East's jack held the first trick. When East followed with the king I decided to win, keeping the 10 of clubs as a possible throw-in card. I followed with ace and king of hearts and from the fall of the cards it seemed likely that the suit would be 4–2. At this point I exited with my third club. East cashed two more clubs and we arrived at this position:

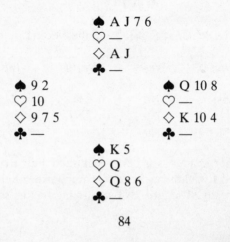

♠ A J 7 6
♡ —
◇ A J
♣ —

♠ 9 2   ♠ Q 10 8
♡ 10   ♡ —
◇ 9 7 5   ◇ K 10 4
♣ —   ♣ —

♠ K 5
♡ Q
◇ Q 8 6
♣ —

84

East exited with a diamond to the jack. I cashed the ace of diamonds, crossed to the king of spades, and led the queen of hearts, squeezing East.

My partner said, 'Well done, but couldn't you have tested the hearts by cashing the queen earlier on?' Funnily enough, this would be a mistake, because then the dummy would have an inconvenient discard on the last club. If dummy comes down to ♠ A J 7 alone East can exit with a spade and South still has to lose a diamond.

They reached four spades at the other table, so we lost one match point.

POINTS TO REMEMBER

1. The point my partner raised about the bidding was that over his two spades I could have bid three clubs to see if he could rebid the spades; if not, I could follow with 3NT.

2. Suppose I had held up the ace of clubs until the third round; then, despite the combined 28 points, I would have had no play for the contract. Players are so used to holding up their controls in notrump contracts that they sometimes forget that the object of this is to exhaust the other opponent of the suit. When the player with the long suit is marked with all the high cards it is generally better to win before the last round and keep a possible exit card.

27 Ugly Duckling

Everyone knows that 5–3–3–2 hands are suitable for play at notrumps and that 5–4–3–1 should usually be played in a suit contract. But what about 4–4–4–1 and 5–4–2–2? I am strongly of the opinion that 4–4–4–1 is primarily a defensive type. I never open light with this holding and I am happy if opponents buy the contract, because I know that no suit is going to break well for them.

5–4–2–2 is more difficult to classify. I once heard Adam Meredith describe this as the 'ugly duckling' of suit combinations. The reason why I remember this remark, made about 25 years ago, is that soon after I spoke of 5–4–2–2 as the 'ugly duck', and I couldn't understand why everyone laughed.

As you will see from the bidding of the following hand, the Polish champion, Kudla, evidently distrusts 5–4–2–2 for notrump contracts. He was playing, at Venice, with Jessero.

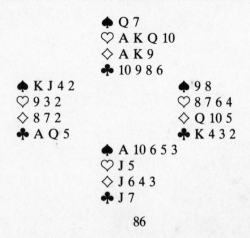

```
                    ♠ Q 7
                    ♡ A K Q 10
                    ◇ A K 9
                    ♣ 10 9 8 6
  ♠ K J 4 2                      ♠ 9 8
  ♡ 9 3 2                        ♡ 8 7 6 4
  ◇ 8 7 2                        ◇ Q 10 5
  ♣ A Q 5                        ♣ K 4 3 2
                    ♠ A 10 6 5 3
                    ♡ J 5
                    ◇ J 6 4 3
                    ♣ J 7
```

Kudla was South and the bidding went:

South	West	North	East
—	—	1♣	No
1♠	No	2NT	No
3♦	No	3♠	No
4♠	No	No	No

Most South players raised to 3NT on the second round. Perhaps Kudla thought to himself, 'If partner has something like K Q x in diamonds and only a single stop in hearts, we will be better off in the suit than in notrumps.' North, it seems to me, with such a strong holding in the fourth suit, could have bid 3NT over three diamonds, but he may have been anxious about the clubs.

Most North–South pairs made 3NT easily enough, so to obtain a fair score South had to make his rather poor contract of four spades. He was off to a good start when West, not unnaturally, began with a heart. The declarer took four rounds of the suit, discarding two clubs. West ruffed the fourth round and rather foolishly (a diamond was indicated) advanced the ace of clubs. South ruffed and used the two diamond entries to ruff two more clubs. This left:

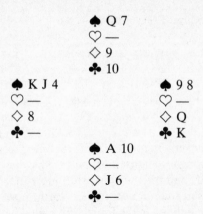

```
              ♠ Q 7
              ♡ —
              ◇ 9
              ♣ 10
♠ K J 4                    ♠ 9 8
♡ —                       ♡ —
◇ 8                       ◇ Q
♣ —                       ♣ K
              ♠ A 10
              ♡ —
              ◇ J 6
              ♣ —
```

South exited with a diamond to East's queen. East made the best play now—a trump. Reading the position correctly, Kudla went up with the ace and led his last diamond, thus making dummy's queen of trumps *en passant*. Making four spades produced a better than average score.

POINTS TO REMEMBER

1. In general, I agree with Meredith's contention that 5–4–2–2 hands play better in the suit (assuming 5–3) than in notrumps. However, on the present hand I would have bid 3NT as South on the second round. Most players are going to finish in 3NT, and when your partner is a first-class player you should be happy, at pairs, to let him play in the popular contract.

2. The most interesting point in the play, I think, was West's lead of a club when he had seen declarer discard two clubs. Players often do this, with a sort of better-late-than-never philosophy, but obviously, when declarer has taken discards in a suit, he is quite prepared for this suit to be led. A diamond from West would have been a much stronger defence.

You won't get far at this game unless, whenever something slightly unexpected has happened, you ask yourself, 'Why did he do that?' On this deal from rubber bridge East made a play that seemed to make the declarer's task easier. South failed to work out why.

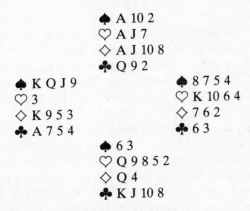

North–South were vulnerable and North opened 1NT. The South hand will by no means always produce a game opposite a 15–17 notrump, and a tournament player would probably adopt a non-forcing sequence such as two diamonds, transfer, followed by 2NT. However, such methods are not usually played at rubber bridge and South on this occasion responded three hearts, which his partner raised to four.

West led the king of spades. Declarer won with the ace and led a club to the king. West won and played two more rounds of spades, South ruffing. A heart was led to the jack and king, leaving the cards as follows:

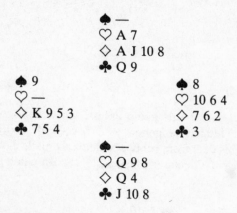

♠ —
♡ A 7
◇ A J 10 8
♣ Q 9

♠ 9
♡ —
◇ K 9 5 3
♣ 7 5 4

♠ 8
♡ 10 6 4
◇ 7 6 2
♣ 3

♠ —
♡ Q 9 8
◇ Q 4
♣ J 10 8

After some thought East led a spade at this point. South raised his eyebrows and took the force in dummy, discarding his possible diamond loser. When the ace of hearts was cashed, West showed out. The declarer's only hope now was to find East with two more clubs; as the cards lay, East was able to ruff the third club and the contract was one down.

When East led a spade after the king of hearts, the declarer should have thought to himself, 'East may be a bit of an ass at the game, but he wouldn't have given me a ruff-and-discard if he had held the king of diamonds.' So to discard a diamond was silly; instead, South must throw a club, while still ruffing in dummy. Then the ace of hearts reveals the trump distribution. No matter, South crosses to the 10 of clubs, takes three rounds of diamonds, and at trick 12 has ♡ Q 9 over East's 10 6.

The defenders were well pleased with themselves, but they had made a mistake too. Did you notice this at the time? Do you see it now?

POINTS TO REMEMBER

1. East was wrong to capture the jack of hearts with the king. Players are always ready to hold up when they hold A x x x in the

trump suit and K x x x is really much the same. If East had held up the king, South would probably have played the ace from dummy, and after this there is no play for the contract. (South can succeed at double dummy, I know; when the jack of hearts wins, he can cross to hand with a club, play four rounds of diamonds, and end-play East.)

2. Even when there is no possibility of establishing a long trump, it is usually right to hold up with K 10 x x in a position of this kind:

```
                  A Q 7
         x                      K 10 8 x
                  J 9 x x x
```

When South plays a low trump to the queen, East's best card is the 8. There is a good chance now that declarer will return to hand and follow with the jack on the next round, hoping to pin a doubleton 10 8 or, perhaps, to avoid losing two tricks to West's possible K 10 x x.

29 Greek Gift

I wonder how, as South, you would have played this hand from rubber bridge? I should tell you that Zia Mahmood was West and I was East.

```
              ♠ 10 9 8 5
              ♡ 3 2
              ◇ 4 2
              ♣ A K 10 6 5
   ◇ K led
              ♠ K Q J 7 4
              ♡ A Q J
              ◇ J 7 6
              ♣ 4 2
```

The bidding has been simple:

South	West	North	East
1♠	No	3♠	No
4♠	No	No	No

West leads the king of diamonds and follows with the queen. East overtakes and returns the 7 of hearts. What now?

Well, you may suspect a trap, but I'm pretty sure that at the table you would have gone up with the ace of hearts and led the jack of diamonds, intending to discard a heart from dummy. Quite a good player did this at the table. The full hand was:

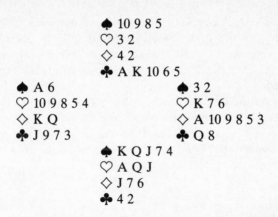

♠ 10 9 8 5
♥ 3 2
♦ 4 2
♣ A K 10 6 5

♠ A 6
♥ 10 9 8 5 4
♦ K Q
♣ J 9 7 3

♠ 3 2
♥ K 7 6
♦ A 10 9 8 5 3
♣ Q 8

♠ K Q J 7 4
♥ A Q J
♦ J 7 6
♣ 4 2

King of diamonds, queen of diamonds overtaken, heart from East; seeing the chance for a discard, you go up with the ace and lead the jack of diamonds. Unlucky! West ruffs and you have gone down in a simple contract.

Two questions arise: what induced East to play this defence, and was the declarer wrong to refuse the heart finesse?

To take East's problem first, I was naturally aware that I might be setting up declarer's jack of diamonds, but to defeat the contract I had to find my partner with at least one trick in the major suits and I could see, of course, that declarer would not be able to take his discard on ♦ J before drawing trumps. Still, I freely admit that in some cases my line of play would have been a mistake. For example, if South had held ♠ A Q J x x and ♥ A J 10, I would have given him a chance to make the contract.

The declarer's problem is more interesting. Is it possible that the jack of diamonds will stand up? Not really, because if West had held, say, ♦ K Q x and the king of hearts he would have led a low diamond at trick two, not the queen. This was perhaps one of those situations—there are many—where the right play is easier to find against strong opponents than against weak ones.

POINTS TO REMEMBER

1. The success of a defender's play on this type of hand depends very much on *tempo*. My own style, both at rubber

93

bridge and duplicate, is to play at an even, but fairly quick, pace. I am not incapable of analysis when the play is difficult, but I know very well that declarers are far more likely to make mistakes when the defenders give no indication that they have a problem.

2. Note the final sentence of the analysis above to the effect that the play is sometimes easier against good opponents than against bad ones. Here South should have paid me the small compliment of thinking, 'Has Martin given me the only chance to make this contract?'

30 A New Vienna Coup

Ever since the earliest days of contract there have been fine players in Austria. The reason why they are not more famous is that it is often impossible for Austria to send any team, let alone its best team, to the European championship. However, some very strong players from Austria take part in the Philip Morris events. Berger and Minel won the Düsseldorf heat one year. This was one of their hands:

```
              ♠ K Q 2
              ♡ A 5 3
              ♢ A J 3
              ♣ K 10 8 2
♠ J 10 8 7                    ♠ 5
♡ K Q                         ♡ 10 9 7 6
♢ K 10 9 6 5                  ♢ 7 2
♣ 5 4                         ♣ A Q J 9 7 6
              ♠ A 9 6 4 3
              ♡ J 8 4 2
              ♢ Q 8 4
              ♣ 3
```

With Minel North and Berger South, the bidding went:

South	West	North	East
—	—	1NT	3♣
3♠	No	4♠	No
No	No		

95

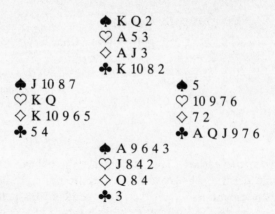

West led the 5 of clubs, East won and returned a trump. Winning in dummy, South ruffed a club and followed with ace and another spade to dummy's queen. Then he ruffed another club and was overruffed. West exited with the king of hearts, won by dummy's ace, and the position was now:

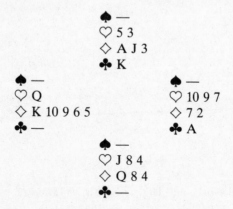

Realizing that his best chance was to find West with KQ of hearts alone, South exited with a low heart to the queen. West had to lead a diamond now and on the third round of this suit East was squeezed in hearts and clubs.

I held the West cards at another table and there the play

developed rather more luckily for the defence. Again a club was led to the 8 and 9, but now East returned the 7 of diamonds. South had shown both majors during the bidding, so one discard would not help him and there was a chance that I might hold ♢ K Q. North won this trick with the jack and later I found myself on play, just as the other West had been. I was able to exit with the *king* of diamonds, however, so that although South made three tricks in diamonds he was in the wrong hand for a squeeze.

POINTS TO REMEMBER

1. As I remarked in my earlier book, I have no good opinion of weak jump overcalls. Here East was not vulnerable, but the jump to three clubs was risky in two ways: he might encounter a 500 penalty when there was no certain game for the opposition; and, much more serious, if opponents played the contract they would be warned of the distribution. To my mind, it is silly even to overcall with two clubs.

2. My partner's diamond return at trick two was not obvious but was certainly the best play. A trump might have killed J x x x in my hand, and a heart could be a mistake in several ways. The diamond gave nothing away and it was quite possible that an early attack on this suit would be good for the defence.

31 The Useful Fifth

Sometimes you will hear players discussing the best way to open 4–4–4–1 or 4–4–1–4 hands. 'I show both majors,' one will say, another 'I open one heart,' a third 'I bid the minor, giving partner a chance to respond in a four-card major.' If you are playing with a partner who prefers five-card majors you must open the minor, but in general I am influenced by the quality of the suits. I don't mind bidding a major such as A K x x, but I would conceal a suit with tenaces, such as K J 9 x.

On this hand from an early round of the Gold Cup, South at one table opened one heart. West overcalled with one spade and South soon finished in four hearts.

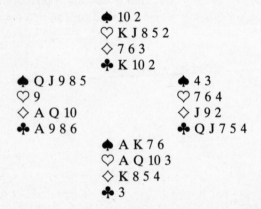

West led the queen of spades, won by the ace. South tried a low club at trick two. West went up with the ace and led the jack of spades. South cashed one heart, ruffed a spade high, returned to the queen of hearts and ruffed his fourth spade. After king and another club he arrived at this position:

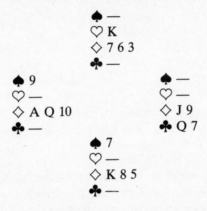

South ruffed the last spade and led a diamond from the table. East had the wit to go up with the jack and the contract was one down.

At the other table I was South and might have opened either one spade or one diamond. I chose one diamond and the bidding continued:

South	West	North	East
1 ◇	1 ♠	dble	No
3 ♡	No	4 ♡	No
No	No		

Partner's negative double of one spade promised (in principle) four hearts, so I was well worth a jump to three.

West led a spade, as before, and I began with three rounds of trumps, West discarding one club and one spade. Now a club was won by the ace and West led another spade. After ruffing a spade I played king and another club, arriving at this position:

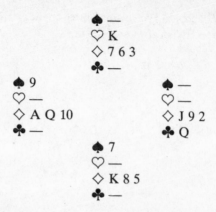

The cards were much the same as in the previous diagram, but the lead was in my hand. I simply exited with my losing spade and discarded a diamond from dummy, leaving West on play.

This was my plan from the first, but it occurred to me afterwards that West could have made the play more difficult—probably impossible—by keeping all his spades. Not so easy, that.

POINTS TO REMEMBER

1. It is quite wrong to determine in advance that with such-and-such distribution you will open a particular suit. For example, with two minor suits such as A Q 9 x and K x x I will generally open the weaker suit, especially if I expect eventually to play in notrumps. I have found it very effective, too, to open one spade on distribution such as 3–1–4–5. Sometimes you steal the opposition's best suit; sometimes you will play in notrumps and escape a dangerous lead; sometimes you will play in spades, probably with a 4–3 fit, and the opponents will let you take ruffs in the short hand.

2. Certainly it was not easy for West, on the present hand, to discard two clubs early on and keep all his spades. I have an idea that this type of defence is more effective than any of us realize, and I intend to look out for it in future.

32 Still a Chance

No doubt you have read about, even if you have not played, hands where it is possible to avoid a trump loser when one opponent has J x x and the other Q x. It is possible, too, to lose only one trick when a defender holds A 10 8 x sitting over the Q 9, or similar, in a position like this:

$$
\begin{array}{c}
\text{K J x} \\
\text{A 10 8 7} \qquad \qquad — \\
\text{Q 9 x x x x}
\end{array}
$$

South discovers the trump position when he leads low to the king. If, after that, he can shorten his own hand twice and end by leading a plain card from dummy, ruffed with the queen, he will leave West on play. I have seen positions like that once or twice, but what about this trump holding:

$$
\begin{array}{c}
\text{Q 2} \\
\\
\text{A J 6 5 4 3}
\end{array}
$$

Must the declarer lose a trump trick? Most players would say yes, but look at this deal:

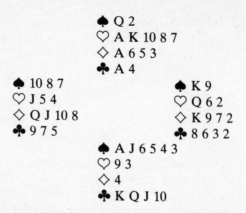

Giorgio Belladonna showed me this hand on the beach of the Lido in Venice. After a miscalculation in the bidding he ended in seven spades. West led a diamond, won by the ace. I think that at the table most players would try the queen of trumps, hoping for some sort of miscalculation on East's part. But there's another way. Suppose you ruff a diamond at trick two and continue with a trump reduction until you arrive at this ending:

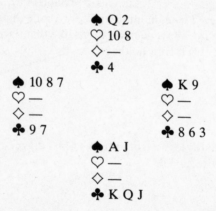

You play three rounds of clubs, and even if your opponents are Forquet and Garozzo they won't be able to prevent you from making the grand slam!

1. When I was first shown this hand I thought that a trump lead would beat the contract. But it doesn't! The declarer plays for this ending:

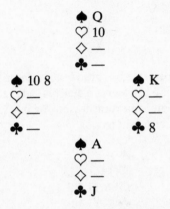

South leads the jack of clubs and the defenders are dead.

2. Such contracts are not to be recommended, obviously, but surprising results can be achieved by avoiding a direct attack on the trump suit. For example, if you can end with A x of the trump suit in hand, Q 10 in dummy, you need lose only one trick to West's K J 9 8, so long as your plain cards are in different suits.

33 Not Sorry, Partner!

After the rather remarkable grand slam described in the last example you may like to observe a deal played in a modest 1NT. It contains, I think, an important lesson for pairs players. These were the North–South hands:

```
                    ♠ 8 7
                    ♡ J 6
                    ◇ A Q 7 6 3
                    ♣ A Q 10 2
    ♡ 4 led
                    ♠ J 6 4
                    ♡ Q 5 3
                    ◇ K J 9 8
                    ♣ J 7 4
```

With East–West vulnerable, North opened one diamond and my response of 1NT bought the contract. West led the 4 of hearts and East played off ace, king and another. After this rather fortunate start I had seven tricks on top, with the possibility of nine or ten if I chose to risk the club finesse.

The obvious course, you may think, is to take seven tricks, for plus 90 must be a better than average score. To my partner's dismay, however, I took four diamond tricks, noting that they were 3–1, then ran the jack of clubs. This lost, and I was one down.

'You must have miscounted your tricks,' said North crossly. 'You had seven tricks on top.'

But on this occasion, at least, I knew what I was doing. Do you see why it was good play, in a pairs, to finesse the club?

Obviously North–South have done well to buy the contract at 1NT, and furthermore the defence has not been dynamic. South should reflect on these lines: 'Most East-West pairs will buy the contract in spades or hearts. If the king of clubs is right for them, they will make 140 or 170, possibly even 620. So it won't help me to record plus 90. But suppose they get to three hearts or three spades, or higher, and have to lose two or three clubs as well. In that case many North–South pairs will score 100. Again, it won't help me to record plus 90; I must play for a better score.'

As it turned out, the full hand was:

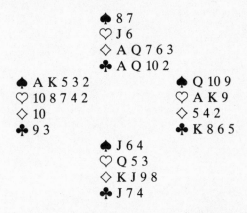

At other tables East–West entered the bidding and registered either 170 or 620, so minus 50 was an excellent score for my side.

POINTS TO REMEMBER

1. Certainly it was feeble of East–West to let non-vulnerable opponents steal the contract in 1NT. They had three opportunities to enter. East could have doubled the opening one diamond; this, I agree, would be over-zealous. Over South's 1NT West could have entered with two diamonds, implying length in the majors. And when 1NT came round to him, East should have risked a double; he might have walked into a 500 penalty, but such risks must be taken.

2. When you are not vulnerable, against vulnerable oppo-

nents, there tends to be little difference between plus 90 and minus 50. When opponents have the balance of the strength, as they had on this occasion, you must aim for a better score than plus 90. It won't make any difference if you go one down.

34 Delayed Action

When I spoke to Giorgio Belladonna on the beach at Venice before the start of the 1980 tournament, he seemed his old ebullient self after his recent illness. He didn't rate his chances of doing well in the tournament very high, but he told me he enjoyed his bridge much more now that the pressure was not on him. This relaxed mood didn't stop him from coming a close third out of 500 pairs and also leading an inexperienced team into third place out of more than 100 teams. This was one hand that he played with his usual skill:

```
                    ♠ A J 5 2
                    ♡ A J 9 7 5
                    ◇ 6 3
                    ♣ A 6
   ♠ K 4                           ♠ Q 10 9 8
   ♡ 2                             ♡ 8 4 3
   ◇ A K Q J 9 7 5                 ◇ 10 2
   ♣ 9 7 3                         ♣ Q 10 8 5
                    ♠ 7 6 3
                    ♡ K Q 10 6
                    ◇ 8 4
                    ♣ K J 4 2
```

With North–South vulnerable the bidding went:

South	West	North	East
No	4 ◇	dble	No
4 ♡	No	No	No

South could have passed the double, but Belladonna preferred to play for the vulnerable game. West cashed two diamonds, then switched to a low club. This was annoying for the declarer, whose first idea had been to duck a spade and play to squeeze East in the black suits. This was impossible now, because the defenders could break up the entries by leading a second club.

Declining the free finesse, Belladonna won the club switch in dummy and played four rounds of trumps. He arrived at this position, with the lead in dummy:

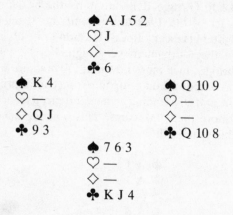

On the last heart East was squeezed. Obviously he cannot afford a club, and if he throws a spade South will discard ♣4, cross to ♣J, and lead the 6 of spades. If West goes up with the king South will win with the ace and clear the suit, making the last two tricks with ♠7 and ♣K.

POINTS TO REMEMBER

1. Most players treat a double of four clubs or four diamonds as 'two-way'. At rubber bridge, or in match play, it would probably be wise for South on the present hand to pass the double and take a medium penalty. At pairs the decision is more difficult. The penalty won't be more than 500, and this may be a moderate result when your side is vulnerable. So on the whole the odds favour the try for game.

2. There was another possible line of play after the club switch. South might have won in hand, drawn two trumps, crossed to the ace of spades, and cashed the ace of clubs; he returns with a third trump, cashes king of clubs, and end-plays West by leading a low spade. But West, of course, can defeat this line by disposing of the king of spades at a timely moment; also, Belladonna's play would have succeeded even if East had held both king and queen of spades.

35 Zero Hour

One of my favourite partners is Lazi Beresiner. Lazi would be the first to say that he was not a player of the highest class, but we have gained many successes together; at Marbella one year, playing with two ladies, we won the teams of four, beating a Swedish team that contained four world-famous players.

We did well again in the Venice tournament. On this deal, I must admit, I underestimated Lazi's dummy play:

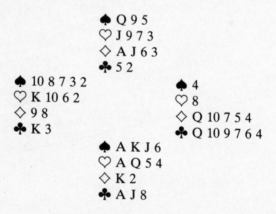

♠ Q 9 5
♡ J 9 7 3
◇ A J 6 3
♣ 5 2

♠ 10 8 7 3 2
♡ K 10 6 2
◇ 9 8
♣ K 3

♠ 4
♡ 8
◇ Q 10 7 5 4
♣ Q 10 9 7 6 4

♠ A K J 6
♡ A Q 5 4
◇ K 2
♣ A J 8

Lazi was South and the bidding was simple:

South	West	North	East
2NT	No	3♣	No
3♡	No	4♡	No
No	No		

West led the 3 of spades. South won in dummy and finessed the queen of hearts, losing to the king. West exited with the 9 of diamonds, which ran to the declarer's king.

Now the obvious continuation is the ace of hearts, but Lazi played low to dummy's jack. He looked a little taken aback when East showed out, and I thought to myself, 'Oh dear, he's chucked a trick in the trump suit, it's going to be a zero.'

Oh ye of little faith! Lazi played a second round of spades, then a diamond to the ace. Two more spades were played and a club was thrown from dummy. Ace of clubs and a club ruff came next, and the position was now:

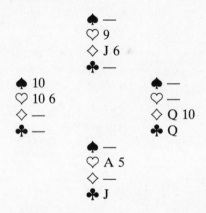

After a few anxious moments Lazi led a diamond from dummy, ruffed with the ace of hearts, and advanced the jack of clubs. A furious West could make only one more trick. This type of ending is known as the *coup en passant*.

POINTS TO REMEMBER

1. Most players made only ten tricks on this hand. Leading the ace of hearts on the second round and finding the 4–1 distribution, they tried unsuccessfully to take a diamond ruff. West overruffed and led a third trump, leaving the declarer with a loser in clubs. (Can South do better after leading the ace of hearts? At double dummy he could lead a low club and

eventually squeeze East in the minor suits.)

2. On the first round of trumps, you will remember, South led low to the queen and West won with the king. In this type of position it is almost always better defence to hold up the king. There are several ways now in which South may lose an extra trick. He may even lead the jack of hearts from dummy on the next round, playing West for 10 x. I made a similar point, you may remember, on deal no. 28.

36 Expensive Gesture

'What did you do on board 24?' Schmuel Lev asked me after a
pairs event in Israel. 'It was the one where South held six spades
to the ace-king.' He was referring to this hand, dealt by West at
love all:

```
                    ♠ Q 10 4
                    ♡ A 7 6 5 4
                    ◇ Q 7
                    ♣ A K 2
   ♠ 6 3 2                        ♠ J
   ♡ J 9 3                        ♡ Q 10
   ◇ 9 6 5 3                      ◇ K J 10 8 4
   ♣ 10 5 4                       ♣ Q J 9 8 6
                    ♠ A K 9 8 7 5
                    ♡ K 8 2
                    ◇ A 2
                    ♣ 7 3
```

'We weren't ambitious,' I said. 'I was North and our bidding
went like this.'

South	West	North	East
—	No	1♡	No
1♠	No	2♠	No
3♡	No	4♣	No
4◇	No	4♠	No
No	No		

113

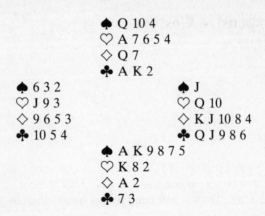

```
              ♠ Q 10 4
              ♡ A 7 6 5 4
              ♢ Q 7
              ♣ A K 2
♠ 6 3 2                        ♠ J
♡ J 9 3                        ♡ Q 10
♢ 9 6 5 3                      ♢ K J 10 8 4
♣ 10 5 4                       ♣ Q J 9 8 6
              ♠ A K 9 8 7 5
              ♡ K 8 2
              ♢ A 2
              ♣ 7 3
```

'It was just as well we didn't try for a slam, because West led a low diamond. My partner did his best. After the diamond had been covered by the queen and king he drew two trumps, eliminated the clubs, cashed two hearts and led a diamond from dummy. East eventually played low, so we just made five. It was a poor result, because six was made at some tables.'

'We bid six and made it,' Lev informed me. 'This was the bidding:

South	West	North	East
—	No	1♡	2NT
3♠	No	4♠	No
5♢	No	6♠	No
No	No		

'West led a low diamond. I played *low* from dummy. You see what that led to? Like your partner, I drew two rounds of trumps, eliminated the clubs, and cashed two hearts, arriving at this position:

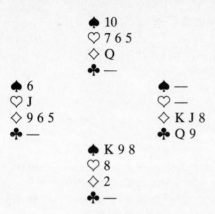

♠ 10
♡ 7 6 5
◇ Q
♣ —

♠ 6
♡ J
◇ 9 6 5
♣ —

♠ —
♡ —
◇ K J 8
♣ Q 9

♠ K 9 8
♡ 8
◇ 2
♣ —

'Now the queen of diamonds left East on play. I thought you might be interested because I know you don't think much of the unusual notrump.'

POINTS TO REMEMBER

1. Lev was quite right: I think that the unusual notrump, as a defensive measure on moderate hands, is wholly misconceived. Here, as so often, the only effect was to suggest a line of play that would not otherwise have occurred to the declarer.

2. Obviously a slam is worth bidding on the North–South cards, and in a sense we were lucky not to be in six spades. It is a mystery to me why players do not force on a hand as good as South's. Only 14 points? What's wrong with that, when you have a good suit, a fit with partner, and three and a half quick tricks? Culbertson pointed out years ago that you do *not* save time or space by responding at the one-level on a hand of this type.

37 Marked Man

Since the beginning of time it has been customary to open the bidding either on quite good hands or on weaker hands containing a long suit. There is no special logic in this style and in ten years' time it may be normal, at any rate for tournament players, to open the bidding on weak balanced hands. Already there have been experiments in this direction. A Polish pair in the mid 1970s caused some amusement by passing, in first or second position, on strong hands of 17 points or so; partner, in third or fourth position, was obliged to open on upwards of 5 points.

The next logical step was to open consistently on weak hands. Thus in the 1981 European Championship John Collings and Paul Hackett played a system in which they consistently opened the bidding on 0–8 points and passed on 9–12. As the critics were quick to point out, this method gave unusual information to opponents who bought the contract. However, there was not much evidence of opponents making much use of the information. This deal from Britain's match against Luxembourg was an occasion when the declarer might have benefited.

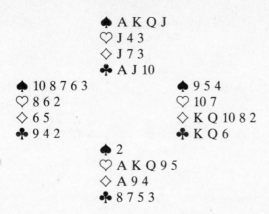

♠ A K Q J
♡ J 4 3
◇ J 7 3
♣ A J 10

♠ 10 8 7 6 3
♡ 8 6 2
◇ 6 5
♣ 9 4 2

♠ 9 5 4
♡ 10 7
◇ K Q 10 8 2
♣ K Q 6

♠ 2
♡ A K Q 9 5
◇ A 9 4
♣ 8 7 5 3

East was the dealer at game all. The British pair reached the normal contract of six hearts and West led a diamond to the 10 and ace. South played the hand in normal fashion. He won with the ace of diamonds, drew trumps, and discarded two diamonds on dummy's spades. Then he ruffed a diamond and played for the club honours to be divided; no luck, one down.

At the other table East passed—which meant that he had 9–12 points, because with anything less he would have opened one club. (Later, in the world championship, the system was changed, to make one diamond the opening on weak hands.) Thus, when South became the declarer in six hearts, he knew that East held the outstanding strength. However, he didn't make the best use of the information. After winning the diamond lead he drew trumps and took two discards on the spades, arriving at this position:

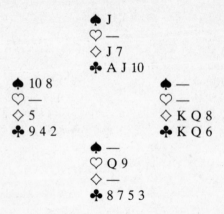

♠ J
♡ —
◇ J 7
♣ A J 10

♠ 10 8   ♠ —
♡ —   ♡ —
◇ 5   ◇ K Q 8
♣ 9 4 2   ♣ K Q 6

♠ —
♡ Q 9
◇ —
♣ 8 7 5 3

On the jack of spades East threw a diamond, and now there wasn't much that South could do. He discarded a club, ruffed a diamond, and finessed ♣J. After ruffing the next diamond he was left with a loser in clubs.

Knowing that all the minor suit honours were held by East, what could South have done? It is simple in a way—he must lead a fourth round of trumps earlier on. The end position is then:

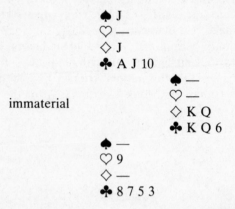

♠ J
♡ —
◇ J
♣ A J 10

immaterial   ♠ —
                ♡ —
                ◇ K Q
                ♣ K Q 6

♠ —
♡ 9
◇ —
♣ 8 7 5 3

Now what can East do when the jack of spades is led? If he throws a diamond, South ruffs a diamond and end-plays East in clubs.

1. The ending above is unusual, but the declarer can rely on general principles. Since he has no intention of taking two finesses in clubs, there is no need to keep two entries, and it must be right to play off all the trumps but one. East will then be subject to pressure when the fourth spade is cashed.

2. In the world championship Collings and Hackett played a pass in the first three positions to show 9–12 points, any distribution, one diamond to show either 0–8, or 12–20 with four clubs, or any 20–22. In the opinion of the captain, Gus Calderwood, the system was not, on balance, a success. It may be that a slightly different style should be adopted against top-class opponents, who will have had time and patience to work out counter-moves.

38 The End Play That Wasn't

Holding

♠ K J 9 7 6
♡ 7 6
♢ 4
♣ A Q J 5 4

as dealer at love all, would you open one club or one spade? There is not a lot in it, but on minimum hands like this I prefer one spade. If partner is not strong, you have a better chance to buy the contract, because opponents will not overcall so readily at the two-level. Opening one spade on the hand below turned out well, though not for the reason I have been discussing.

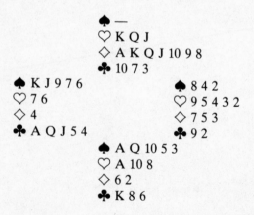

I opened one spade as West and the bidding soon went sky-high:

South	West	North	East
—	1♠	dble	No
3NT	No	5◇	No
6NT	No	No	No

North had no good reason to take out 3NT, and South's 6NT looks doubtful to me, as his spade honours were on the wrong side of the opening bid.

I led the 7 of hearts and declarer began to run off the diamonds. It is very important on such occasions to form an early plan—not just to make the easy discards and then start thinking. Since South obviously held the outstanding high cards, I could count him for eleven tricks and I could see the danger of being thrown in and forced to lead from ♠KJ into the AQ.

The best defence on such hands depends on the calibre of the opposition. A first-class declarer will expect a strong opponent to discard in a deceptive way, perhaps keeping a singleton king. It may then be best for the defender to play a straightforward game, keeping the obvious cards. On the present occasion South was no champion and the fact that I had opened one spade made it easy for me to pretend that my distribution was 6–2–1–4. I began by throwing 7, 6, J of spades, followed by 4 of clubs. The position was then:

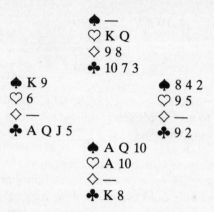

```
              ♠ —
              ♡ K Q
              ◇ 9 8
              ♣ 10 7 3
♠ K 9                         ♠ 8 4 2
♡ 6                           ♡ 9 5
◇ —                           ◇ —
♣ A Q J 5                     ♣ 9 2
              ♠ A Q 10
              ♡ A 10
              ◇ —
              ♣ K 8
```

On the next two diamonds I threw the 9 of spades, followed by the 5 of clubs. On the last heart I discarded the queen of clubs and now South, down to ♠AQ and ♣K, triumphantly (!) exited with the king of clubs. I won with the ace and produced the jack, trying not to look too happy.

POINTS TO REMEMBER

1. The opening one spade turned out well on this occasion, because it was natural for South to take me for six spades and four clubs. Most of the textbooks advise an opening one club with 5–5 in the black suits, but I prefer one spade on most weak or medium hands.

2. Remember the point I made about its being important to form an early picture about the declarer's distribution. With experience you will learn the next step, which is to think without appearing to think! Oh yes, that is important in high-class play. As declarer, I find that a defender's 'trances' often tell me a lot about his hand.

39   Kill the Threat

Few things are more annoying than to see an opponent succeed in an obvious sacrifice bid. Both my partner and myself could have done better on this deal from rubber bridge:

```
                    ♠ J 4 2
                    ♡ 8 6 5 2
                    ◇ 3
                    ♣ A K 6 5 2
  ♠ 7 5 3                          ♠ A
  ♡ A Q 10                         ♡ K J 9 7 3
  ◇ A K 10 7 6                     ◇ 9 8 4 2
  ♣ J 7                            ♣ Q 10 3
                    ♠ K Q 10 9 8 6
                    ♡ 4
                    ◇ Q J 5
                    ♣ 9 8 4
```

East–West were vulnerable and the bidding went like this:

South	West	North	East
No	1 ◇	No	1 ♡
1 ♠	2 ♡	2 ♠	4 ♡
4 ♠	dble	No	No
No			

West, my partner, led the ace of diamonds and switched to a trump. What should I have returned? Well, I dare say you would have done the same as I did: I played back a heart and West led a

123

second round of trumps. Declarer won in hand and led the queen of diamonds, which was covered and ruffed. Now a heart was ruffed, and already my heart began to sink. After two more trumps and the jack of diamonds the position was:

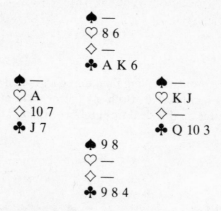

South led the 9 of spades and discarded a club from the table. I threw a club, knowing that it was useless. Declarer cashed the top clubs in dummy and returned to hand to make his tenth trick with the 9 of clubs.

We could have defeated this trump squeeze in a number of ways. West could have killed the heart menace by switching to ace and another heart at trick two. When in with the ace of spades, I might have risked a club; and certainly when my partner won the heart lead he should have led a club. For this type of trump squeeze dummy needs two entries; South can do nothing if clubs are attacked early.

POINTS TO REMEMBER

1. The deal illustrates the special characteristic of a trump squeeze. East controlled both the danger suits, clubs and hearts, and no ordinary squeeze would be possible because he would be playing after the dummy. But the three clubs in the South hand were a menace, also, and it was essential to destroy one of dummy's entries. Imagine that a round of clubs had been played:

124

then the penultimate trump would not embarrass East, who would be able to throw a heart.

2. No doubt most defenders would have done much the same as we did. West thought that a second round of trumps would prevent a diamond ruff, and if South had been 6–1–4–2 the trump continuation would have been the best defence.

In match play some hands are flat, with no possibility of a swing, but in a pairs just one extra trick may make a big difference. This deal from a tournament in Zurich is an example:

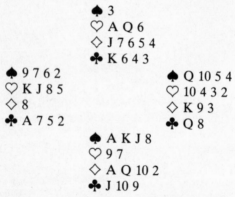

South was the dealer at love all. Almost all the North–South pairs finished in 3NT and made ten or eleven tricks. When the Austrian pair of Rohan and Feichtinger were North–South, Rohan opened 1NT and his partner raised to game. Personally I don't like opening a strong notrump with a plain doubleton in a major suit, but Rohan explained to me that for some reason there was no other way to bid the hand in his system.

Most West players led a low spade against 3NT, but on this occasion West, following the old notion of 'fourth best from your longest and strongest suit', began with a low heart. In a team game the declarer might possibly play low from dummy, but in a pairs, where the object is to make more tricks than the rest of the field, it is certainly right to go in with the queen. When this held,

Rohan led the jack of diamonds from dummy, unblocking the 10 when East played low. On the five rounds of diamonds West discarded three spades and one club. Declarer took the spade finesse and cashed the ace, to arrive at this position:

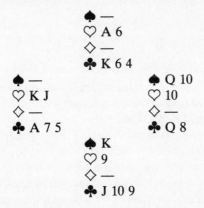

On the king of spades West discarded a club and North the 6 of hearts. Then a club to the king and a club back gave the declarer twelve tricks and an undisputed 'top'.

Well played by South, but has anything struck you about the end game? Look again. Yes, West had a chance to win the brilliancy prize by discarding the ace of clubs on the king of spades! Then South is held to eleven tricks.

POINTS TO REMEMBER

1. West led the 5 of hearts against 3NT, remember, and I remarked that declarer in a team game might possibly play low from dummy. Why just 'possibly'? Because if you apply the Rule of Eleven, East has only one card higher than the 9, and this can hardly be the king since with J 10 8 x West would have led the jack. So it is right in any circumstances to go in with the queen.

2. For West to discard the ace of clubs in the end game would be a small calamity if East's clubs were J x instead of Q x. But only a small calamity, because for declarer to make thirteen tricks instead of twelve would make very little difference to the score.

127

41 Carbon Copy

Players often discuss the relative ability of men and women at bridge, and often they make ridiculous statements. The situation is perfectly clear, I think. There are a few, but very few, women who have a natural gift equal to that of the best men. Who, after all, has a quicker grasp of the play than Rixi Markus? On the other hand, many women become very good players, provided that they have the opportunity to play with a top-class partner. For example, Lee Dupont would not claim to be a natural genius at the game, but from playing often with Garozzo she has become a very fine performer. See how she handled this deal from the open pairs at Venice:

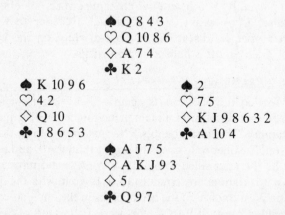

```
              ♠ Q 8 4 3
              ♡ Q 10 8 6
              ◇ A 7 4
              ♣ K 2
♠ K 10 9 6                    ♠ 2
♡ 4 2                         ♡ 7 5
◇ Q 10                        ◇ K J 9 8 6 3 2
♣ J 8 6 5 3                   ♣ A 10 4
              ♠ A J 7 5
              ♡ A K J 9 3
              ◇ 5
              ♣ Q 9 7
```

East opened three diamonds at game all and the bidding continued:

South	West	North	East
—	—	—	3◇
dble	No	4◇	No
4♡	No	No	No

West led the queen of diamonds to dummy's ace. Most players made just ten tricks, losing two spades and a club, but Lee had a different idea. She began by ruffing a diamond, crossing to dummy with a trump, and ruffing the last diamond. When the trumps fell on the next round she led a low club to the king and ace, leaving East on play in this position:

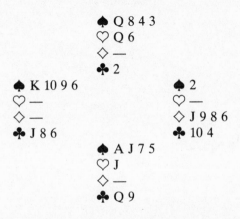

When East exited with a club, South won with the queen, ruffed the 9, and led a spade to the jack and king. Now West was end-played, forced to lead a spade at the cost of a trick or to concede a ruff-and-discard.

It would have made no difference if East, in the diagram position, had exited with a spade. West plays the 9, dummy wins, and after the queen of clubs and a club ruff West is thrown in.

POINTS TO REMEMBER

1. Many players would not—did not—see the possible advantage of taking diamond ruffs in the closed hand. Nothing is lost

if the trumps are 3–1, and if they are 2–2 then declarer has chances to gain a trick from the elimination play.

2. After Benito had congratulated her, Lee asked whether she could have made the contract if the 8 and 6 of spades had been exchanged. 'You can,' he answered, 'but you have to be in your own hand at the finish. Say that you draw trumps, then knock out the ace of clubs. East's best return is a club. You ruff the third club, ruff a diamond, and lead a low spade to the queen. Then you can ruff the last diamond—not necessary as the cards lie— and exit with a low spade.'

42 Museum Piece

Many double-dummy problems and, for that matter, many reported brilliancies, depend on unblocking plays, cleverly foreseen. In my experience, such hands seldom occur at the table, or, if they do, the point is not seen until too late. I can recall only one hand where I saved a trick by this kind of play, and even then I still went 500 down! This was the hand, with East the dealer at game all:

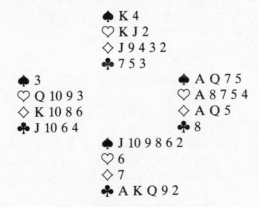

I was South and the bidding went:

South	West	North	East
—	—	—	1♡
1♠	2♡	No	4♡
4♠	No	No	dble
No	No	No	

I don't say that my four spades was a great call; sometimes partner is short in clubs and you find you could have beaten four hearts. However, it was rubber bridge, my partner was a good player, and I wanted to keep the rubber going.

West led the 10 of hearts, covered by the jack and ace. East switched to the 8 of clubs and I won with the ace. The jack of spades lost to the queen and now East led the ace of diamonds and followed with the queen.

Something warned me to ruff this trick with the 6 of spades, not the 2. Then I led the 8 of spades to the king and ace. The position was now:

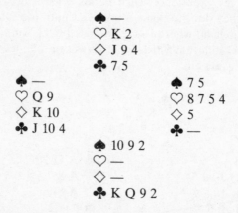

East led another diamond, and with a fairly clear idea now of what I was trying to do, I ruffed with the 9 of spades, cashed the 10, and exited with the 2, to arrive at this ending:

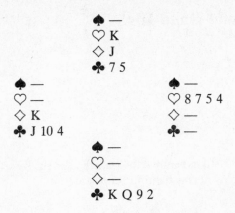

```
                    ♠ —
                    ♡ K
                    ◇ J
                    ♣ 7 5
    ♠ —                         ♠ —
    ♡ —                         ♡ 8 7 5 4
    ◇ K                         ◇ —
    ♣ J 10 4                    ♣ —
                    ♠ —
                    ♡ —
                    ◇ —
                    ♣ K Q 9 2
```

East was obliged to lead a heart and West was caught in a suicide squeeze. My manoeuvre had saved only one trick and I was still 500 down, but I was quite pleased!

POINTS TO REMEMBER

1. I said above that 'something warned me' to ruff the second diamond with the 6 of spades, not the 2. I don't mean that I had some sort of inspiration: it is normal technique to keep possible cards of exit, though of course it seldom makes any difference.

2. As my partner remarked later, it would probably have made no difference if I had ruffed the second diamond with the 2 of spades. Imagine that in the end game I had held 10 9 6 of spades instead of 10 9 2. If I had ruffed with the 9 and followed with the 10, would East have thought of dropping the 7? Probably not!

43   Second Hand High

In the big Christmas event at the Manchester Bridge Club almost every pair played this hand in four hearts:

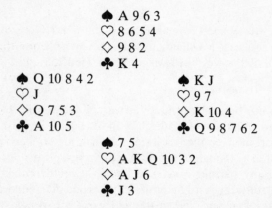

```
            ♠ A 9 6 3
            ♡ 8 6 5 4
            ◇ 9 8 2
            ♣ K 4
♠ Q 10 8 4 2            ♠ K J
♡ J                    ♡ 9 7
◇ Q 7 5 3              ◇ K 10 4
♣ A 10 5               ♣ Q 9 8 7 6 2
            ♠ 7 5
            ♡ A K Q 10 3 2
            ◇ A J 6
            ♣ J 3
```

North dealt and South opened one heart in third position. As East–West were vulnerable, some West players passed, others came in with one spade, but in any event North raised to two hearts and South finished in game.

At my table we were fairly lucky. West overcalled in spades, East ventured three clubs, and West began with ace and another club. My partner drew trumps, then played ace and another spade, leaving East on lead in this position:

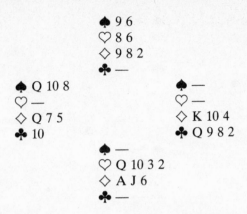

```
                    ♠ 9 6
                    ♡ 8 6
                    ◇ 9 8 2
                    ♣ —
♠ Q 10 8                          ♠ —
♡ —                              ♡ —
◇ Q 7 5                          ◇ K 10 4
♣ 10                             ♣ Q 9 8 2
                    ♠ —
                    ♡ Q 10 3 2
                    ◇ A J 6
                    ♣ —
```

At this point East had to attack diamonds. Obviously the 10 would not be a good choice, but which is better—the king or a low one? Most players would choose the king, and that is what East did here. However, my partner took the right view; he won with the ace, crossed to dummy, and ran ◇ 8. What would have happened if East had led ◇ 4? It's tricky, because South might reason along the lines, 'With K 10 x or Q 10 x East would probably have led high. Perhaps he has K Q x?'

At other tables West led a low spade against four hearts. Suppose that East wins with the king and returns a spade. Declarer's best line now is to ruff a spade with the 10 of hearts, draw trumps, and lead a club. West must win and exit with a club. South ruffs dummy's last spade, crosses to ♡ 8, and leads ◇ 8 from the table in this position:

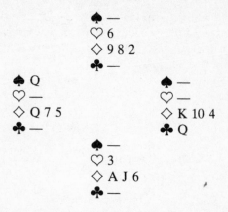

```
              ♠ —
              ♡ 6
              ◇ 9 8 2
              ♣ —
  ♠ Q                        ♠ —
  ♡ —                        ♡ —
  ◇ Q 7 5                    ◇ K 10 4
  ♣ —                        ♣ Q
              ♠ —
              ♡ 3
              ◇ A J 6
              ♣ —
```

For East to cover the 8 with the 10 may not be good enough. South plays the jack, West wins, and when the 5 is returned South will probably make the right guess. But if East covers the 8 with the king, declarer has no chance.

POINTS TO REMEMBER

1. In the first example, did you note my partner's play of ace and another spade? Since West had bid spades and had not led them, he could not hold a strong sequence. Playing ace and another, instead of just ducking the first round, was quite likely to create a situation in which the defenders would be forced to lead diamonds.

2. The diamond holding on this deal gives rise to various possibilities. In most cases the best play for a defender who holds, say, K 10 x or Q 10 x over the 9 or the 9 8 is to play the high card on the first round. This is another instructive situation of the same sort:

```
                     A J 6
           Q 10 5             K 8 4
                     9 7 3
```

Most players in West's position, if they had to open this suit, would lead the 10. This may not be good enough: East covers the

136

jack with the king and on the return of the 4 declarer may guess right. West must lead the queen, and even if South can return to his hand for the next lead, the defence will take two tricks.

44   To the Cleaners

On this deal from a pairs event Colin Simpson and I were playing against two of Britain's most promising young players, Tony Forrester and John Armstrong. Both have already played for Britain in the European Championship. I dare say it does me little credit, but I do enjoy taking a young pair 'to the cleaners', as the saying goes.

```
                    ♠ A 9 7
                    ♡ K Q 8 6
                    ◇ K J 10 7
                    ♣ 7 5
   ♠ 10 6                        ♠ K Q 5 3
   ♡ A J 7 5                     ♡ 10 3 2
   ◇ 9 8 5 2                     ◇ A Q
   ♣ J 10 3                      ♣ A K Q 9
                    ♠ J 8 4 2
                    ♡ 9 4
                    ◇ 6 4 3
                    ♣ 8 6 4 2
```

With East–West vulnerable the bidding went:

South	West	North	East
Forrester	Simpson	Armstrong	Hoffman
—	—	1NT	dble
2♣	dble	No	No
2♠	No	No	dble
No	No	No	

138

West led the jack of clubs against two spades doubled and switched to a low spade at trick two. I won with the queen and returned the 3. South does best at this point to win with the jack and lead a heart, but in practice he played low and the 10 forced dummy's ace. I won the next trick with ♣ Q, cashed the king of spades, and made the top clubs. This left:

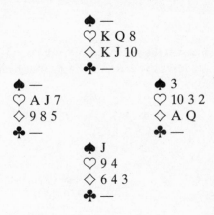

♠ —
♡ K Q 8
♢ K J 10
♣ —

♠ —
♡ A J 7
♢ 9 8 5
♣ —

♠ 3
♡ 10 3 2
♢ A Q
♣ —

♠ J
♡ 9 4
♢ 6 4 3
♣ —

I exited with the 10 of hearts, which ran to dummy's queen. Now the declarer was in deep trouble. If he leads a diamond I cash the second diamond and put partner in for a diamond ruff, and a heart return from dummy is no better. We took 900 for a clear top.

POINTS TO REMEMBER

1. West did not have much for his double of two clubs on the first round, but in these situations (*a*) a double is co-operative, saying 'I like it if you do', and (*b*) players in the South position often bid two clubs on a short suit, intending to rescue themselves if doubled.

2. When doubled in two clubs South would have been wiser to redouble and pass a take-out into two diamonds. It is always dangerous, with a weak hand, to rescue oneself into spades, which may mean finishing at the three-level.

45   Discovered Late

How would you assess the prospects of six diamonds on the deal below? There is a loser in hearts and East's four trumps seem to create a problem.

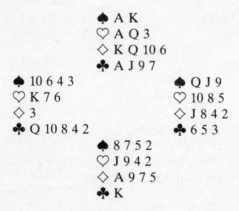

♠ A K
♥ A Q 3
♦ K Q 10 6
♣ A J 9 7

♠ 10 6 4 3   ♠ Q J 9
♥ K 7 6   ♥ 10 8 5
♦ 3   ♦ J 8 4 2
♣ Q 10 8 4 2   ♣ 6 5 3

♠ 8 7 5 2
♥ J 9 4 2
♦ A 9 7 5
♣ K

First I will describe the play when our opponents were in six diamonds. West led a club, which ran to the king. Declarer finessed the queen of hearts and followed with ace and another. West won and exited with a spade. The position was then:

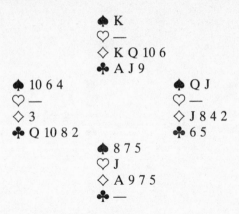

♠ K
♥ —
♦ K Q 10 6
♣ A J 9

♠ 10 6 4
♥ —
♦ 3
♣ Q 10 8 2

♠ Q J
♥ —
♦ J 8 4 2
♣ 6 5

♠ 8 7 5
♥ J
♦ A 9 7 5
♣ —

Declarer played off king and queen of diamonds. Although he seemed, in a way, to have plenty of tricks, the communications were awkward and it was impossible to make the contract.

At my table my partner opened two clubs and though I held an ace and a king it seemed advisable to respond two diamonds. North bid 2NT, non-forcing in Acol, and I bid three clubs, asking for four-card suits. My partner showed four diamonds and we were soon in the slam.

Again, West led a club to the king and at trick two I finessed the queen of hearts. The ace of hearts stood up, and then I set about a cross-ruff, which seemed reasonably safe since West was marked with the long clubs. After cashing ace and king of spades I played ace of clubs and ruffed a club, then ruffed a spade with ♦10. I had not lost any trick so far and the position was:

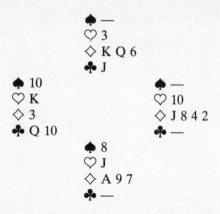

The jack of clubs was ruffed by ◇7, East discarding a heart. Then I ruffed a spade with ◇Q and it wasn't difficult to take two more tricks with the ace and king of trumps!

POINTS TO REMEMBER

1. Every textbook contains the lesson, 'Draw trumps unless there is a good reason not to.' Good players, I think, are in less of a hurry to draw trumps than average players. They may occasionally run into an unexpected ruff and look rather foolish, but on many more occasions they learn about the distribution as they go along.

2. There were good reasons on the present hand for playing on cross-ruff lines. East's failure to cover the 7 of clubs at trick one indicated that West had led from long clubs. After the first two tricks in hearts it was plain that West held at least three hearts to the king. It was fairly safe to ruff the third spade in dummy because if West had held five spades, in addition to three hearts and long clubs, the hand would have been unmanageable.

46 More Deadly than the Male

I first met the Austrian player, Maria Kirner, at Juan-les-Pins several years ago. Since then she has represented Austria's open team in the European Championship. So it was no surprise when with Dieter Sims she won a big pairs event in Venice, defeating many famous international players. When I asked her for a hand she said rather vaguely, 'Well, there seemed to be four losers on this hand I played in four spades, but one of them just disappeared.'

```
                    ♠ 9 6 4 3
                    ♡ K J 7 6
                    ◇ 8 3
                    ♣ A Q 3
    ♠ A J 8                         ♠ 7 2
    ♡ Q 9 8 5                       ♡ 10 4 3 2
    ◇ K J 7 2                       ◇ 10 6 5
    ♣ K 6                           ♣ J 10 8 4
                    ♠ K Q 10 5
                    ♡ A
                    ◇ A Q 9 4
                    ♣ 9 7 5 2
```

South was the dealer at love all and the bidding went:

South	West	North	East
1◇	dble	redble	1♡
1♠	No	3♠	No
4♠	No	No	No

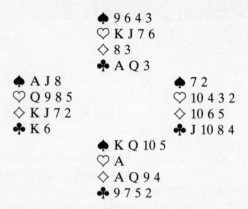

♠ 9 6 4 3
♡ K J 7 6
◇ 8 3
♣ A Q 3

♠ A J 8
♡ Q 9 8 5
◇ K J 7 2
♣ K 6

♠ 7 2
♡ 10 4 3 2
◇ 10 6 5
♣ J 10 8 4

♠ K Q 10 5
♡ A
◇ A Q 9 4
♣ 9 7 5 2

West led the 5 of hearts to declarer's ace. At trick two Maria led the king of trumps, and after a slight hesitation West played low. A club was led to the queen, and the king of hearts was cashed, South discarding a diamond. A heart ruff was followed by a club to the ace and the last heart was ruffed with the 10 of trumps. The position was now:

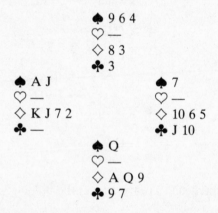

♠ 9 6 4
♡ —
◇ 8 3
♣ 3

♠ A J
♡ —
◇ K J 7 2
♣ —

♠ 7
♡ —
◇ 10 6 5
♣ J 10

♠ Q
♡ —
◇ A Q 9
♣ 9 7

South exited with the queen of spades and after making his two trump tricks West was obliged to lead a diamond. The contract would have been safe if West had held three clubs and had unblocked the king, because then the fourth club would have provided a discard for dummy's diamond loser.

POINTS TO REMEMBER

1. You may think that North's raise to three spades, following a redouble, was on the forward side; but his honours were well placed, over the strong hand, and his partner had made a free rebid. At my table North, after a similar sequence, bid only two spades; wisely, as it turned out, because his partner succeeded in making only nine tricks.

2. Did you pick out the mistake made by the defenders at Maria's table? It was difficult to foresee, certainly, but West would have done better to capture the king of spades with the ace and exit with the king of clubs. Declarer can ruff two more hearts but is then in the wrong hand for an end play against West.

47 Saved by the Bell

Neither side is vulnerable and in fourth position you hold:

♠ Q 8
♡ Q 10 4
♢ K 8 2
♣ A 10 7 3 2

Playing in a multiple team event, what action would you take after three passes? You'd throw it in? Very wise, but in this type of event even a small gain may be important, and I ventured 1NT. Not so clever, for the full hand was:

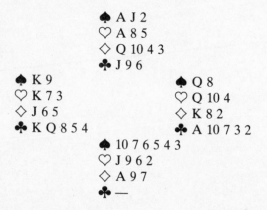

♠ A J 2
♡ A 8 5
♢ Q 10 4 3
♣ J 9 6

♠ K 9
♡ K 7 3
♢ J 6 5
♣ K Q 8 5 4

♠ Q 8
♡ Q 10 4
♢ K 8 2
♣ A 10 7 3 2

♠ 10 7 6 5 4 3
♡ J 9 6 2
♢ A 9 7
♣ —

My partner might have opened the bidding, and so might North, but neither did. West raised 1NT to 3NT, naturally, and South began with a low spade. It is normal to play the king from dummy on such occasions, because if South holds the ace he may not know that East's queen is going to drop. North headed the king with the ace and returned the jack. When I led clubs, North dropped the jack on the first round to emphasize that he held the ace of hearts. Making no mistake, South discarded two diamonds and three hearts, and I finished an undignified three down.

It seemed a minor disaster, because even if our other pair registered 140 in spades we would still lose the board. (A difference of 10 points counts as a tie only when both sides have scored 'below the line'.) However, we were due for a surprise because at the other table, where Sheehan and Mahmood held the North–South cards, they registered 170 in a spade part-score. West began with the king of clubs and Zia ruffed. A diamond went to the 10 and king, and East led another club. The declarer crossed to the ace of trumps, ruffed the last club, and played two more diamonds. This left:

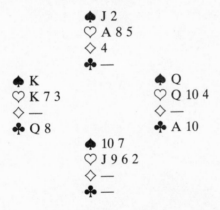

♠ J 2
♡ A 8 5
◇ 4
♣ —

♠ K
♡ K 7 3
◇ —
♣ Q 8

♠ Q
♡ Q 10 4
◇ —
♣ A 10

♠ 10 7
♡ J 9 6 2
◇ —
♣ —

South exited with a trump and now West had to open up the hearts or concede a ruff-and-discard. When a low heart went to the queen and the 4 of hearts was returned, Zia played low and so ended with ten tricks.

POINTS TO REMEMBER

1. Despite the result at my table, I think the opening 1NT, at

this form of scoring, was correct. It would, of course, be foolish to open one club, giving opponents an easy chance to overcall. The final result, three down in 3NT with a combined 23-count, was freakish.

2. You may think that it was very risky play by Zia to lead a trump in the end game shown above. The point is that good players acquire a very good sense of what is happening on a deal of this sort. When you buy the contract at a low level with a combined count of 17 you can be very sure that the cards are evenly divided against you. There was a strong probability here that both opponents had 5–3–3–2 distribution, for otherwise they would surely have been more active in the bidding.

48 The King Falls

It is a well-known fact that beginners and moderate players enjoy taking a finesse, whereas good players will go a long distance to avoid it. (Sometimes they go too far, spurning a simple finesse for an imaginary squeeze.) On this deal from a pairs tournament at Dusseldorf the two Tonys, Forrester and Sowter, scored a game by avoiding a finesse that at the beginning of the hand must have seemed the natural play.

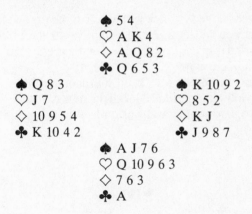

The bidding was simple:

South	North
1♡	2♢
2♡	4♡
No	

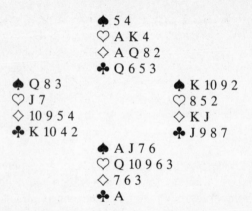

♠ 5 4
♡ A K 4
◇ A Q 8 2
♣ Q 6 5 3

♠ Q 8 3
♡ J 7
◇ 10 9 5 4
♣ K 10 4 2

♠ K 10 9 2
♡ 8 5 2
◇ K J
♣ J 9 8 7

♠ A J 7 6
♡ Q 10 9 6 3
◇ 7 6 3
♣ A

Not liking to lead from his clubs or spades, West began with the 7 of hearts. In a way this was a lucky lead, because if a trump is not led South can ruff two spades and still not lose a trump trick.

Declarer won the first trick with the 10 of hearts and led a low spade. East won and led a second trump. South played a spade to the ace, ruffed a spade, and returned to the ace of clubs to draw the outstanding trump.

The problem now was to keep the diamond losers to one. South led a low diamond and ducked the trick to East's jack. East cashed his spade winner and was on lead in this position:

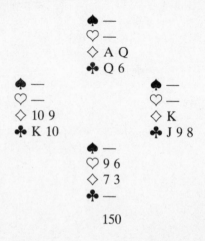

♠ —
♡ —
◇ A Q
♣ Q 6

♠ —
♡ —
◇ 10 9
♣ K 10

♠ —
♡ —
◇ K
♣ J 9 8

♠ —
♡ 9 6
◇ 7 3
♣ —

When East exited with a club South ruffed and led his last heart, on which West threw a diamond and dummy a club. Now a diamond was led at trick twelve, West followed with the 10, and Forrester went up with the ace to drop East's king.

Why play for the drop? It wasn't too difficult, really; South had already committed himself to the view that West held the king of clubs, and as this had to be his last card a finesse of $\diamond$Q could hardly succeed. This type of play goes by the name of 'show-up squeeze'.

POINTS TO REMEMBER

1. West, you may recall, led the 7 of trumps from J7. It turned out to be quite a good lead here, because it prevented dummy from taking two ruffs, but in general a lead from Jx or Qx should be avoided. Players who make this lead hope to make an unexpected trick when the declarer has a suit headed by AK10. It is true that if partner has the corresponding Qx or Jx declarer may think of finessing on the second round, so losing an 'impossible' trick. Far more often, in my experience, the lead from Jx or Qx will surrender a trick that the defence might otherwise have made.

2. The chance for a 'show-up' or 'discovery' squeeze occurs whenever the defender in front of a possible finesse is obliged to keep a protecting card in another suit. In *Squeeze Play Is Easy* Terence Reese and Patrick Jourdain give a pretty hand where the spade distribution is:

$$\text{A Q x x}$$
$$\text{10 x x x x} \qquad \qquad \text{K}$$
$$\text{J x}$$

West has to keep the controlling card in another suit, so at the finish the declarer, with no initial indication about the lie of the spade suit, is able to drop the singleton king.

151

49 Lifeline

This is another deal from the big Christmas event at the Manchester bridge club. It wasn't difficult to make 3NT on the North–South cards, so for a fair score South had to aim at ten tricks.

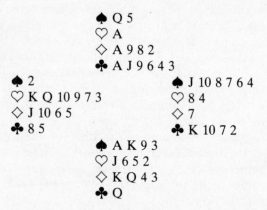

```
                    ♠ Q 5
                    ♡ A
                    ◇ A 9 8 2
                    ♣ A J 9 6 4 3
    ♠ 2                             ♠ J 10 8 7 6 4
    ♡ K Q 10 9 7 3                  ♡ 8 4
    ◇ J 10 6 5                      ◇ 7
    ♣ 8 5                           ♣ K 10 7 2
                    ♠ A K 9 3
                    ♡ J 6 5 2
                    ◇ K Q 4 3
                    ♣ Q
```

At my table Steve Lodge, who has already played for Britain in the Bermuda Bowl and surely has a great future, opened as West with a multi-coloured two diamonds. The usual meaning of the 'multi' is a weak two in one of the majors. The bidding continued:

South	West	North	East
Hoffman	Lodge	Simpson	Sowter
—	2◇	No	2♡
No	No	3♣	No
3NT	No	No	No

West led the king of hearts to dummy's ace and I began by playing ace and another diamond. It was a slight surprise to find that West had the long diamonds, but at least this meant that any pair in six diamonds would fail. I followed with the queen of clubs, which ran to East's king, and East returned his second heart. Though he knew the hearts were not breaking, Steve decided to cash the queen and hold me to ten tricks.

It may seem that West could have saved a trick by exiting with the jack of diamonds, but it would have been easy enough for me to organize an end play against East, forcing him to lead into dummy's AJ9 of clubs.

At another table the winners of this event, Chris Dixon and Victor Silverstone, also played in 3NT after a similar auction. In dummy with the ace of hearts Chris led a low club to the queen, then cashed the king of diamonds. This left:

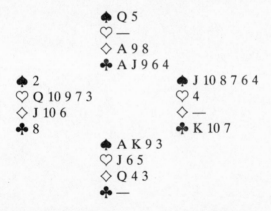

```
                    ♠ Q 5
                    ♡ —
                    ♢ A 9 8
                    ♣ A J 9 6 4
    ♠ 2                              ♠ J 10 8 7 6 4
    ♡ Q 10 9 7 3                     ♡ 4
    ♢ J 10 6                         ♢ —
    ♣ 8                              ♣ K 10 7
                    ♠ A K 9 3
                    ♡ J 6 5
                    ♢ Q 4 3
                    ♣ —
```

Now the declarer made a very neat and unexpected play: he exited with a low heart!

Consider West's position. If he leads a heart or a diamond he presents declarer with a tenth trick. A spade forces East to split his honours, exposing him to an end play. After some thought West exited with a club. South now had enough entries to set up the club suit, losing just one heart and two clubs.

153

1. Note that at both tables East played high-low on the original heart lead. The bidding had marked South with a guard in the suit, and on such occasions it is right for a defender to indicate length by playing high-low from a doubleton, lowest from three small.

2. You remember South's lead of a low heart at the second table? I described this as neat and unexpected, but it is not an unusual move for expert players. When you know that one defender has a comparatively weak hand it is good tactics to cut the link between the opposing hands by leading the only suit where they have communication.

50 Waiting for Godot

Looking at the deal below, you will see that South has four losers in spades—two clubs and two trumps. But in a rubber game at the Acol club it didn't quite go like that!

```
                    ♠ A Q 5 3 2
                    ♡ A 2
                    ♢ A Q J 8
                    ♣ 9 8
   ♠ K J 10 6                        ♠ —
   ♡ 10                              ♡ Q 9 7 5 4 3
   ♢ 10 9 3 2                        ♢ 7 6 5 4
   ♣ A K 7 3                         ♣ Q 10 2
                    ♠ 9 8 7 4
                    ♡ K J 8 6
                    ♢ K
                    ♣ J 6 5 4
```

West was the dealer at love all and the bidding went like this:

South	West	North	East
—	1♣	dble	1♡
dble	1♠	dble	2♣
No	No	2♢	No
2♠	No	3♠	No
4♠	No	No	No

West cashed ace and king of clubs, then switched to a heart, waiting for two trump tricks, which (like Godot) never arrived.

155

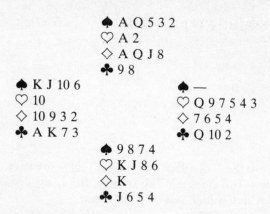

♠ A Q 5 3 2
♡ A 2
♢ A Q J 8
♣ 9 8

♠ K J 10 6
♡ 10
♢ 10 9 3 2
♣ A K 7 3

♠ —
♡ Q 9 7 5 4 3
♢ 7 6 5 4
♣ Q 10 2

♠ 9 8 7 4
♡ K J 8 6
♢ K
♣ J 6 5 4

South won the heart lead and ruffed a third club, noting the fall of the queen. He came back to the king of diamonds and paused to consider the distribution. West was marked with four clubs and there was no reason to suppose that his bid of one spade was a bluff, so presumably he held four spades and, surely, a singleton heart, as otherwise he would not have removed the double of one heart.

Having reached this conclusion, South cashed the jack of clubs, discarding the ace of hearts from dummy. The 7 of spades was covered by the 10 and queen, and three diamonds were cashed. This left:

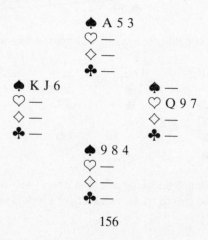

♠ A 5 3
♡ —
♢ —
♣ —

♠ K J 6
♡ —
♢ —
♣ —

♠ —
♡ Q 9 7
♢ —
♣ —

♠ 9 8 4
♡ —
♢ —
♣ —

When declarer led a low spade to the 8, West played the 6. 'Nobody end-plays me,' he remarked.

1. While complimenting his partner on the play, North contended that South should have bid 'at least' two spades over East's two clubs. I think, too, that South should have bid one spade in preference to doubling one heart. In general, it is better to show a four-card major than to seek to penalize opponents at the one-level.

2. It wasn't at all easy for West to see what was going to happen, but he might have beaten the contract if, after his partner had played the 10 of clubs at trick one, he had followed with a low club to the queen. Now East must exit with a diamond or a heart, and South, still needing to ruff two clubs and to lead a trump from hand, will not have enough entries.

51 Unhappy Ending

As I remarked in my first book, I remember my bad hands just as much as—indeed, more than—my good ones. See what you make of this deal from the Philip Morris event in Budapest:

　　　　　　　　　　♠ 8 5
　　　　　　　　　　♡ K 4 3
　　　　　　　　　　♢ Q J 3 2
　　　　　　　　　　♣ A K 10 5
♣ Q led
　　　　　　　　　　♠ K Q 9 6
　　　　　　　　　　♡ J 10 9 8 2
　　　　　　　　　　♢ A 8 7
　　　　　　　　　　♣ 2

My partner and I were playing the Blue Club, so when he opened one diamond I responded one spade, my shorter suit. He rebid 1NT, I showed my hearts, and we finished in four hearts. West led the queen of clubs, won in dummy. A spade to the king held the trick and I followed with the 10 of hearts. West went up with the ace and, after some thought, led a diamond. I was happy to win in dummy, East playing the 9. East took the next spade and we were down to:

♠ —
♡ K 4
♢ Q 3 2
♣ K 10 5

♠ Q 9
♡ J 9 8 2
♢ A 8
♣ —

East exited with the 10 of spades. What would you do now? Ruff in dummy, perhaps, and cash the king of hearts? Unlucky, West shows out. If you play king and another club now, the jack falls, but it doesn't help. When East takes his trump trick and exits with a club, you can win with the 10 in dummy, but East still has a trump and you cannot get back to hand to draw it. (East, as you expected, began with a singleton diamond.) I played along these lines and lost the contract, since this was the full deal:

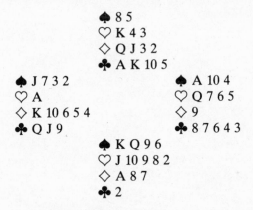

```
              ♠ 8 5
              ♡ K 4 3
              ♢ Q J 3 2
              ♣ A K 10 5
♠ J 7 3 2                    ♠ A 10 4
♡ A                         ♡ Q 7 6 5
♢ K 10 6 5 4                ♢ 9
♣ Q J 9                     ♣ 8 7 6 4 3
              ♠ K Q 9 6
              ♡ J 10 9 8 2
              ♢ A 8 7
              ♣ 2
```

You remember how the play went? Club to dummy, spade to king, heart to ace, diamond from West. (This may look silly, but West may have thought that I had a singleton diamond and that it would help the defence to establish a force.) Spade to ace, another spade from East. Do you see the play now, going back to

159

the second diagram? Declarer must ruff with the *king* in dummy and follow with ♡4. The rest is easy.

1. To ruff the third spade with the king of hearts was not certain to be the right play. Why? Because West might, in theory, have held ♡AQ alone; then he would win the second heart and give his partner a diamond ruff.

2. This possibility did cross my mind, but there were strong indications the other way. First, with ♡AQ alone West would not necessarily have played the ace of trumps on the first lead: it would have been more natural to cover the 10 with the queen. Secondly, there was West's rather dangerous lead of a diamond away from the king. Why had he done this when a spade would have been safe enough? He must have thought there was some chance of establishing a force—as there would have been if I had held a singleton diamond. This, in turn, had to mean that he was placing his partner with four trumps and had a singleton himself.

52 So They Say

The king of clubs is always single—so they say. I suppose we just notice when it happens. Sometimes it's lucky, as on this deal from rubber bridge.

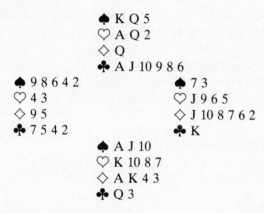

```
                    ♠ K Q 5
                    ♡ A Q 2
                    ◇ Q
                    ♣ A J 10 9 8 6
  ♠ 9 8 6 4 2                      ♠ 7 3
  ♡ 4 3                            ♡ J 9 6 5
  ◇ 9 5                            ◇ J 10 8 7 6 2
  ♣ 7 5 4 2                        ♣ K
                    ♠ A J 10
                    ♡ K 10 8 7
                    ◇ A K 4 3
                    ♣ Q 3
```

I opened 1NT as South and my partner soon carried me to the skies:

South	North
1NT	3♣
3◇	4NT
5♡	5NT
6♡	7NT
No	

My partner said afterwards that he thought my three diamonds

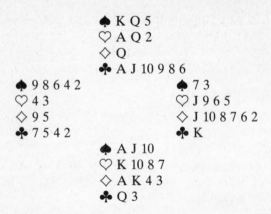

♠ K Q 5
♡ A Q 2
♢ Q
♣ A J 10 9 8 6

♠ 9 8 6 4 2   ♠ 7 3
♡ 4 3   ♡ J 9 6 5
♢ 9 5   ♢ J 10 8 7 6 2
♣ 7 5 4 2   ♣ K

♠ A J 10
♡ K 10 8 7
♢ A K 4 3
♣ Q 3

indicated support for clubs—that with Qx only he would have expected me to bid simply 3NT. Well, that may be his system— it's not mine.

West led a spade and when the dummy went down I uttered the usual 'Thank you, partner'. I might have put the club finesse to the test early on, but you never know, and after winning the first spade I played off three rounds of hearts, followed by a diamond to the queen. After two more spades and the ace and king of diamonds we were down to:

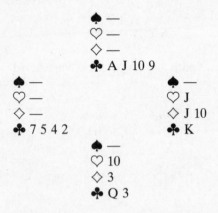

♠ —
♡ —
♢ —
♣ A J 10 9

♠ —   ♠ —
♡ —   ♡ J
♢ —   ♢ J 10
♣ 7 5 4 2   ♣ K

♠ —
♡ 10
♢ 3
♣ Q 3

Since West had shown out on the third heart and the third

162

diamond, it wasn't difficult to count his hand. His last four cards had to be clubs. If K x x x I couldn't pick up the king, so the only chance was to lead the queen and play the ace from dummy. 'I knew you'd play it well,' said my partner smugly.

POINTS TO REMEMBER

1. North, you may remember, used 4NT to ask for aces and 5NT to ask for kings. That style has gone out of fashion among tournament players. When the 4NT bidder knows, from the response, that all the aces are held, he may bid a new suit, saying 'We have the necessary controls, and if you have anything extra there should be enough tricks for seven;' or he may bid 5NT, which means 'We have the four aces, but I have nothing more to show.' To use 5NT to ask specifically for kings is usually wasteful and imprecise. On this occasion Roman Blackwood would have been useful, because the response would have shown two kings of the same colour, so not the king of clubs.

2. An odd point about the hand is that a *heart* lead from West, although it shows up the heart position, would have been excellent for the defence. With ten tricks on top in the other suits, South must surely take the straightforward finesse in clubs. This leads to an interesting thought. There must be occasions when it is right to give an opponent certain information, because this may cause him to abandon a winning line of play.

53   Adventure Story

Playing with Zia Mahmood in a high-stake game is an adventure as well as a pleasure. You never quite know what he will try next, either in the bidding or the play. On the following deal he opened the South hand with one spade, and from then on it was difficult not to finish in four spades. (Obviously 3NT would be a more comfortable spot.)

```
                    ♠ A 10 3
                    ♡ 9 8 7 2
                    ◇ K J 10 8
                    ♣ A 2
  ♠ J 9 8 4                      ♠ Q 2
  ♡ 6 5 4                        ♡ A Q J
  ◇ 5 4 2                        ◇ 6 3
  ♣ 8 6 4                        ♣ Q J 10 9 7 5
                    ♠ K 7 6 5
                    ♡ K 10 3
                    ◇ A Q 9 7
                    ♣ K 3
```

The bidding went as follows:

South	West	North	East
1♠	No	2◇	3♣
3◇	No	4♠	No
No	No		

It looks like one down, doesn't it? Two trumps to lose and two hearts.

164

West led the 4 of clubs—lowest from three—and Zia won in dummy. A low heart was led from the table, East went in with the ace and returned the queen of clubs. South played king and ace of spades, then another heart from dummy to the queen and king. He cashed two diamonds, then exited with a heart to East's jack. The position was now:

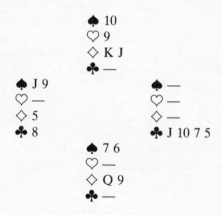

♠ 10
♥ 9
♦ K J
♣ —

♠ J 9   ♠ —
♥ —   ♥ —
♦ 5   ♦ —
♣ 8   ♣ J 10 7 5

♠ 7 6
♥ —
♦ Q 9
♣ —

When East exited with a club Zia ruffed with ♠6 and discarded the king of diamonds from dummy. Then he cashed the queen of diamonds and followed with the 9, making dummy's 10 of spades *en passant*.

It was a dazzling performance and I asked Zia why he had adopted this line. He might have played the trumps to be 3–3, for example. He pointed out that he had an early count of the clubs and also of the diamonds, assuming that West had not false-carded. Also, West had played the 4 and 5 of hearts, so it was likely that East, who had played ace and queen, also held the jack. And if West, after all, had held four hearts? Then East's remaining trump would be the jack and the contract would still be made.

POINTS TO REMEMBER

1. West's opening lead of lowest from three in partner's suit is not the normal British practice, but I am sure it is right. It is often

very important to know whether partner has two small or three small, and low from three is the only way to convey this message on the first lead. The convention known as 'middle-up' from three cards is one of the silliest ever invented: partner doesn't know until too late whether the lead of the 6 is from 8 6 4 or from 6 4.

2. South might have made this contract in any event, but note how West's conventionally correct play in hearts and diamonds and spades helped declarer to count the hand. Many players go through this stage. Bear in mind always that defensive signals are right only when it is more important to inform partner than to deceive the declarer. It is generally right to lead a conventional card, and right also to give an orthodox picture of odd and even holdings when discarding on declarer's long suit. At all other times you must consider whether any signals you choose to give will be more helpful to partner or to the declarer. Generally speaking, the better your partner, the less you will need to give a picture of your hand.

54 Late Arrival

Opening pre-emptive bids are also called shut-out bids, and I suppose the general intention is to prevent opponents from reaching game or slam their way. In these days it seems to happen almost as often that opponents are promoted into a contract they would not otherwise have reached.

```
                    ♠ A 2
                    ♡ A Q 10 9 8
                    ◇ 7 4 3
                    ♣ 6 4 2
    ♠ K J 9 5                      ♠ Q 7 3
    ♡ 5 4 3                        ♡ 2
    ◇ Q 10 8 5                     ◇ J 9
    ♣ J 7                          ♣ K Q 10 9 8 5 3
                    ♠ 10 8 6 4
                    ♡ K J 7 6
                    ◇ A K 6 2
                    ♣ A
```

East opened three clubs at love all and, sitting South, I thought I had just enough to double—for take-out, of course. The bidding continued:

South	West	North	East
—	—	—	3♣
dble	No	4♣	No
4♡	No	6♡	No
No	No		

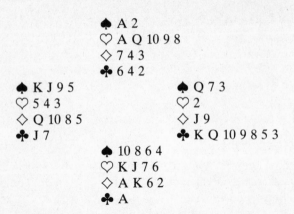

♠ A 2
♡ A Q 10 9 8
♢ 7 4 3
♣ 6 4 2

♠ K J 9 5
♡ 5 4 3
♢ Q 10 8 5
♣ J 7

♠ Q 7 3
♡ 2
♢ J 9
♣ K Q 10 9 8 5 3

♠ 10 8 6 4
♡ K J 7 6
♢ A K 6 2
♣ A

Left to ourselves, we would never have reached this dubious contract. West led a club to the ace and I continued in the obvious fashion—heart to dummy, club ruff, heart to dummy, another club ruff. West, after a little thought, discarded a spade. This left:

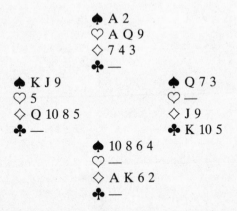

♠ A 2
♡ A Q 9
♢ 7 4 3
♣ —

♠ K J 9
♡ 5
♢ Q 10 8 5
♣ —

♠ Q 7 3
♡ —
♢ J 9
♣ K 10 5

♠ 10 8 6 4
♡ —
♢ A K 6 2
♣ —

I crossed to the ace of spades, drew the outstanding trump, and exited with a spade. No problem now—I was able to set up a long spade and make the contract.

East wasn't pleased. 'Why didn't you throw a diamond instead of a spade?' he asked his partner. This wouldn't have helped, of course. I simply duck a diamond, win the spade or diamond return, and make a long diamond after drawing the last trump.

No, when declarer ruffs the third club with the king of hearts, West must underruff. Typical, I thought; I've been waiting for years to play this coup and now the chance goes to an opponent. After West has underruffed, South plays a spade to the ace and leads a trump, discarding a diamond from hand. This leaves:

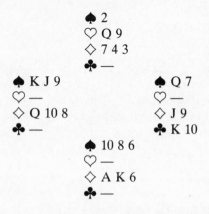

I lead the queen of hearts from dummy, discarding a diamond. West must throw a spade. Now, when I lead a spade, East can go in with the queen and lead a club. Since this takes the last trump from dummy, West can safely throw a diamond and make the last trick with the king of spades.

POINTS TO REMEMBER

1. Although it turned out well, I don't think my partner's bid of four clubs was well judged. If South bids four spades, North has to try five hearts—not very satisfactory. In general, it is wise to aim at plus scores when opponents have pre-empted. North should bid simply four hearts over the double.

2. This is the basic situation for an underruffing coup:

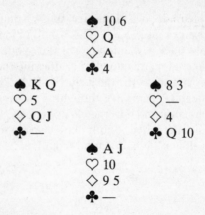

```
              ♠ 10 6
              ♡ Q
              ◇ A
              ♣ 4
  ♠ K Q                    ♠ 8 3
  ♡ 5                      ♡ —
  ◇ Q J                    ◇ 4
  ♣ —                      ♣ Q 10
              ♠ A J
              ♡ 10
              ◇ 9 5
              ♣ —
```

Hearts are trumps, the lead is in dummy, and South ruffs a club with the 10 of hearts. It is clear that West must underruff. The play is effective because West, who is threatened in two suits, plays after South and so cannot be squeezed by the subsequent lead of a trump from North.

55 Foolish Information

What is the silliest mistake often made by good players? I will tell you my opinion: it is the utterly pointless double made by a weak hand when he is strong in a suit bid by opponents who are on their way to a high contract. This example occurred at rubber bridge recently.

```
                    ♠ A Q 9
                    ♡ A 2
                    ◇ K Q 9 8 5
                    ♣ 5 4 3
  ♠ 2                               ♠ 7 5 4
  ♡ Q 10 9 6                        ♡ 8 7 5 4 3
  ◇ J 4 3                           ◇ A 10 7 6
  ♣ K J 9 7 6                       ♣ 2
                    ♠ K J 10 8 6 3
                    ♡ K J
                    ◇ 2
                    ♣ A Q 10 8
```

North–South were a strong pair and the bidding went like this:

South	West	North	East
1♠	No	2◇	No
3♣	dble	3♡	No
3♠	No	4NT	No
5◇	No	6♠	No
No	No		

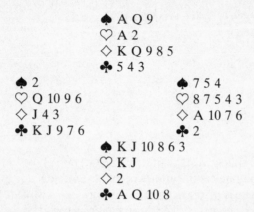

```
                    ♠ A Q 9
                    ♡ A 2
                    ◇ K Q 9 8 5
                    ♣ 5 4 3
♠ 2                                  ♠ 7 5 4
♡ Q 10 9 6                           ♡ 8 7 5 4 3
◇ J 4 3                              ◇ A 10 7 6
♣ K J 9 7 6                          ♣ 2
                    ♠ K J 10 8 6 3
                    ♡ K J
                    ◇ 2
                    ♣ A Q 10 8
```

South would not have pressed for a slam after West's double of three clubs, but his partner took control. West led a heart against six spades and South won with the jack.

The normal way to play this hand, I think you will agree, is to lead a diamond to the queen. If it loses to the ace and a club comes back, South will put in the queen, hoping later to discard two clubs on dummy's diamonds. But this plan didn't look good after West's double of three clubs, which surely marked him with the king of clubs. Still, there was nothing better at trick two than to lead a diamond and see what happened.

When West played low, South reflected that if West held ◇ A x x it would be possible to ruff out the ace and establish two discards. However, this was against the odds and after some thought South inserted the 8 of diamonds from dummy. East won with the 10 and returned his singleton club. South won, played two rounds of trumps, and led the king of diamonds in this position:

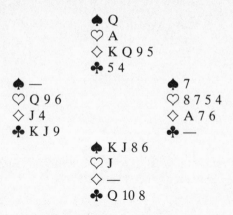

```
                    ♠ Q
                    ♡ A
                    ◇ K Q 9 5
                    ♣ 5 4
    ♠ —                         ♠ 7
    ♡ Q 9 6                     ♡ 8 7 5 4
    ◇ J 4                       ◇ A 7 6
    ♣ K J 9                     ♣ —
                    ♠ K J 8 6
                    ♡ J
                    ◇ —
                    ♣ Q 10 8
```

East covered the king and South made the contract when the jack fell on the next round.

POINTS TO REMEMBER

1. West's double was particularly foolish on this occasion because the odds were that he would have the lead against the final contract. And even if the hand were played by North in 3NT, it might be better for his partner to lead a heart than a club.

2. Doubles of this sort are made more often by the player sitting over the likely dummy. For example, the bidding goes:

South	West	North	East
1♠	No	3♠	No
4♣	No	4◇	dble

East doubles because he has a few diamonds, headed by AQ. But is it wise? Bear in mind, first, that the double increases the number of actions open to South: he can pass, redouble, bid four hearts, or four spades. If South has the king of diamonds he will know this is a trick. If North holds the king of diamonds, or even KJ, he will know that the king has to be protected. As I see it, such doubles give away much more than they stand to gain.

173

56 Double Event

Sometimes a contract is well played at both tables, but in quite a different way. This deal occurred in a team event in Switzerland:

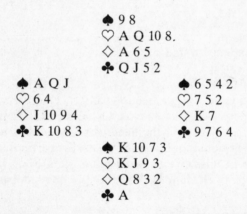

♠ 9 8
♥ A Q 10 8.
♦ A 6 5
♣ Q J 5 2

♠ A Q J   ♠ 6 5 4 2
♥ 6 4   ♥ 7 5 2
♦ J 10 9 4   ♦ K 7
♣ K 10 8 3   ♣ 9 7 6 4

♠ K 10 7 3
♥ K J 9 3
♦ Q 8 3 2
♣ A

Sitting South, I played in four hearts after West had made a take-out double. West led a trump, which turned out to be quite a good choice. I won in dummy and ran the 8 of spades. West won and led another trump. When in on the next round of spades, West led the jack of diamonds to his partner's king, and East returned a diamond, which I won in hand. I ruffed out the ace of spades and drew the trump, to arrive at this position:

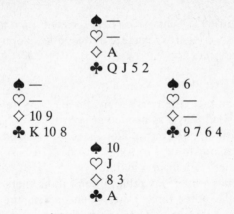

Now I cashed the 10 of spades, then led my last trump. West, who was down to ◇10 9 and ♣K 10, was caught in a criss-cross squeeze.

I thought there might be a chance for a swing, but it didn't turn out that way. South was again in four hearts and this time West led the jack of diamonds. East won and returned a diamond to dummy's ace. A diamond ruff was threatened, so declarer drew three rounds of trumps, followed by queen of diamonds and ace of clubs. The position was then:

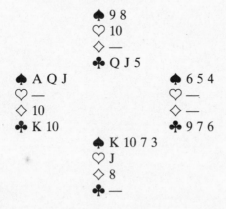

South now exited with a diamond and discarded a spade from

dummy. West tried ace and queen of spades but could not make another trick. A criss-cross squeeze at one table, a pretty loser-on-loser at the other.

1. On the surface there are only three losers in a heart contract, yet good play was needed at both tables to land four hearts. The deal supports my opinion that 4–4–4–1 hands are not good as an attacking force. For some reason, even 4–4–3–2 plays better when there is a fit in a major.

2. As the play went at my table, I don't think there was any defence. At the other table East, when in with the king of diamonds at trick one, should have led back a spade, making use of his only entry. West wins and exits with a diamond. Now South is obliged to draw three rounds of trumps and finds himself a trick short.

57 Whatever Must Be, Must Be

When this deal occurred in a pairs event there was a succession of 50s to East–West. See if you would have done better in the obvious contract of four spades.

                  ♠ A 7
                  ♡ K 8 5 4
                  ◇ 9 7 3
                  ♣ A K 6 2

♡ 10 led

                  ♠ J 10 9 5 4 2
                  ♡ A Q
                  ◇ K 6 4 2
                  ♣ 7

West leads the 10 of hearts and you see that, barring accidents, you can dispose of one diamond on the king of clubs and one on the king of hearts. Then, if the ace of diamonds is on the wrong side, you will need some luck in the trump suit. So you begin by cashing ace and queen of hearts, followed by ace and king of clubs. All follow to the king of hearts, West having played the 10, 7 and 9. You are down to:

♠ A 7
♡ 8
◇ 9 7 3
♣ 6 2

♠ J 10 9 5 4 2
♡ —
◇ K 6
♣ —

You lead a diamond to the king. West wins, cashes the queen, and plays a third diamond; East discards a club and you ruff. Now it's just a matter of finding West with a doubleton honour in spades, is it not? The jack of spades is covered by the queen, but you find that East began with K 8 6 3, so you lose two more tricks. The full hand was:

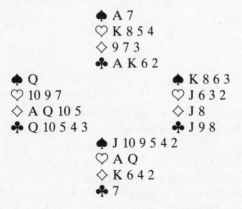

♠ A 7
♡ K 8 5 4
◇ 9 7 3
♣ A K 6 2

♠ Q
♡ 10 9 7
◇ A Q 10 5
♣ Q 10 5 4 3

♠ K 8 6 3
♡ J 6 3 2
◇ J 8
♣ J 9 8

♠ J 10 9 5 4 2
♡ A Q
◇ K 6 4 2
♣ 7

As you see, South could have made the contract if at the finish he had played West for a singleton honour in spades. Was there any reason to do that? Of course there was! These were the last five cards:

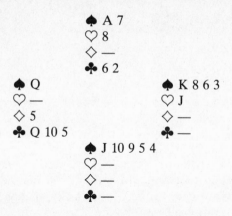

```
              ♠ A 7
              ♡ 8
              ◇ —
              ♣ 6 2
  ♠ Q                    ♠ K 8 6 3
  ♡ —                    ♡ J
  ◇ 5                    ◇ —
  ♣ Q 10 5               ♣ —
              ♠ J 10 9 5 4
              ♡ —
              ◇ —
              ♣ —
```

South cannot be sure of the club position, but what he does know is that East still holds the jack of hearts. So what will happen if South runs the jack of spades and finds West with Qx or Kx? East will win and lead a heart, so the contract will still be defeated. The *only* hope was to play West for a singleton queen or king of spades.

POINTS TO REMEMBER

1. Most players, as the end game approaches, try to work out how the cards lie. The next stage, equally important in many hands, is to work out how the unknown cards *must* lie if you are to make your contract.

2. Would it have been good play for East to drop the jack of hearts under the king, thus concealing the heart distribution? Not on this occasion, because then declarer would discard another diamond on the 8 of hearts and the defenders would lose their chance of making two trumps and two diamonds. But this type of play—discarding the card you are known to hold—is often right.

58   Discovery Play

The Israeli international, Schmuel Lev, used to play a lot of rubber bridge in London and I can tell you that he is a very shrewd operator at the game. I was lucky enough to be his partner when this hand was played:

```
                    ♠ A Q 10
                    ♡ K 10 7
                    ◇ A 8
                    ♣ A J 7 6 5
    ♠ J 5                           ♠ K 3
    ♡ 9 8 6 5 4 3                   ♡ A 2
    ◇ 9 7 5 2                       ◇ K Q J 10 6 4
    ♣ 2                             ♣ Q 10 9
                    ♠ 9 8 7 6 4 2
                    ♡ Q J
                    ◇ 3
                    ♣ K 8 4 3
```

North–South were vulnerable and the bidding went:

South	West	North	East
Lev		Hoffman	
No	No	1♣	2◇
2♠	No	3◇	dble
No	No	4♠	No
No	5◇	dble	No
5♠	No	No	No

180

Deciding against the lead of his singleton club, West began with a low diamond. Lev won in dummy and led a low heart. East went in with the ace and led the king of diamonds, ruffed by declarer.

Not fancying the spade finesse, Lev played a spade to the ace and followed with the king and 10 of hearts. It would have been poor play for East to ruff, and instead he discarded a diamond. South crossed to the king of clubs and the position was then:

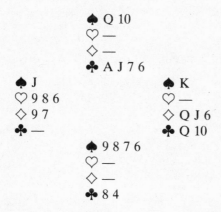

Lev took the right view now, exiting with a trump, which left East on play. Once East had shown up with a doubleton heart and had declined to ruff the third round of the suit, the distribution was clear.

POINTS TO REMEMBER

1. Many players would have lost this contract by ruffing a diamond at trick two and taking a spade finesse. In a contract of this kind, reached after competitive bidding, good players like to 'fish around'. There was no danger in playing on hearts (West could hardly have held seven hearts and four diamonds), and discovery of the 6–2 break made it fairly easy to gauge East's distribution.

2. South's bid of five spades was borderline, it seems to me, and the contract would have been defeated if West had led his

singleton club. But I don't think West was wrong. A singleton lead of declarer's main side suit is always easy to read; it kills partner's Qxx and often helps the declarer to assess the distribution of other suits. It is a lead I choose only when there seems to be no other hope for the defence.

59 The Seven Dwarfs

Most bidding partnerships make a great 'thing' of finding the 4–4 fit in a major; and if the fit does not exist, they give up thoughts of playing in the suit at game level. That is a mistake, because sometimes there is no better game contract. The play on this deal was difficult because I had to accept a force early on.

```
                    ♠ Q 4 3
                    ♡ Q 9 7
                    ◇ K 8 3
                    ♣ Q J 7 4
♠ K 8 2                         ♠ 10 9 5
♡ A K J 10 6                    ♡ 8 5 4 2
◇ 6 4 2                         ◇ A 10 7 5
♣ 6 3                           ♣ 8 2
                    ♠ A J 7 6
                    ♡ 3
                    ◇ Q J 9
                    ♣ A K 10 9 5
```

East–West were vulnerable and the bidding went:

South	West	North	East
1♣	1♡	1NT	2♡
2♠	No	3♠	No
4♠	No	No	No

Sitting South, I was pretty sure my partner held only three spades, partly because he was the type who would normally

183

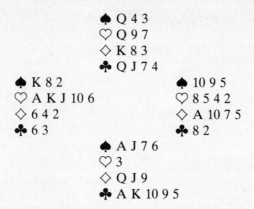

♠ Q 4 3
♡ Q 9 7
◇ K 8 3
♣ Q J 7 4

♠ K 8 2
♡ A K J 10 6
◇ 6 4 2
♣ 6 3

♠ 10 9 5
♡ 8 5 4 2
◇ A 10 7 5
♣ 8 2

♠ A J 7 6
♡ 3
◇ Q J 9
♣ A K 10 9 5

respond in a four-card major and partly because of the tortured way in which he raised to three spades (though on a point of ethics, of course, I had to ignore this).

West led the king of hearts and shifted to the 6 of diamonds. East won with the ace and returned a low heart. As I had lost two tricks already and was sure to lose at least one spade, I had to ruff. Look at the position now:

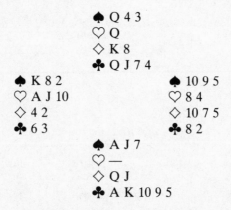

♠ Q 4 3
♡ Q
◇ K 8
♣ Q J 7 4

♠ K 8 2
♡ A J 10
◇ 4 2
♣ 6 3

♠ 10 9 5
♡ 8 4
◇ 10 7 5
♣ 8 2

♠ A J 7
♡ —
◇ Q J
♣ A K 10 9 5

At this point I needed to find the spades 3–3, and funnily enough I had to find West with the king, not East. (Suppose I cross to dummy and finesse the jack of spades successfully: I am

184

no better off.) In practice, I led the jack of spades from hand. West won with the king and played another heart. Now I was able to ruff, cash the ace of spades, and cross to dummy to draw the remaining trumps.

POINTS TO REMEMBER

1. There is nothing magical about making ten tricks with a trump suit divided 4–3. The present hand was awkward because I was obliged to ruff early on in the hand containing the four trumps. I think most players would agree that a 3–3 break occurs more often than the mathematical 36 per cent. This is sometimes attributed to imperfect shuffling, but I think the real reason is that the 5–1 and 6–0 breaks can be excluded when the opponents have been comparatively quiet in the auction. As between 4–2 and 3–3, the odds are then about 57 to 43.

2. It would have been good play for West to hold up his king of spades on the first round, though South can still succeed by following with a low spade. He can then ruff the next heart with the ace and enter dummy to draw the remaining trumps with the queen.

60   Lucky Strike

Sitting West, with neither side vulnerable, you hold:

> ♠ 9 2
> ♡ J 4 2
> ◇ K 10 9 6 5
> ♣ 6 5 3

Your partner opens four spades and the bidding continues:

South	West	North	East
—	—	—	4♠
dble	No	6♣	No
6♡	No	No	dble
No	No	No	

You have to find a lead. Assuming that partner has made a Lightner double, asking for an unexpected lead, you must rule out the obvious suit, spades, and also the trump suit, hearts. Should it be a diamond, or a club, the suit bid by dummy?

Playing in the Two Stars with Marius Wlodarczyk, the experienced British international, Louis Tarlo, reasoned as follows:

'Partner may have doubled for a diamond lead or because he is void of clubs. I think I can have it both ways by leading the *king* of diamonds. If partner holds the ace of diamonds and a void in clubs he will let me hold the lead and play a club at trick two. If by chance he is void of diamonds and holds the ace of clubs, he will ruff the diamond and cash his ace.'

So Louis made the surprising lead of the diamond king and the full hand turned out to be:

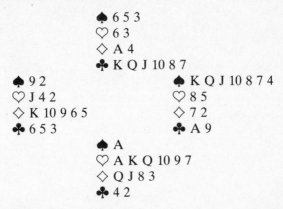

```
                    ♠ 6 5 3
                    ♡ 6 3
                    ◇ A 4
                    ♣ K Q J 10 8 7
    ♠ 9 2                          ♠ K Q J 10 8 7 4
    ♡ J 4 2                        ♡ 8 5
    ◇ K 10 9 6 5                   ◇ 7 2
    ♣ 6 5 3                        ♣ A 9
                    ♠ A
                    ♡ A K Q 10 9 7
                    ◇ Q J 8 3
                    ♣ 4 2
```

The lead was a triumph—but not for either of the expected reasons. With his entry for the clubs knocked out, South tried to ruff the third round of diamonds with the 6 of hearts. 'If I hadn't held the 8 of hearts I wouldn't have doubled,' Marius remarked afterwards.

POINTS TO REMEMBER

1. Was the double of six hearts a sound idea? East might say, 'Well, I don't suppose the bidding will go like this at many tables. If they make six hearts we're going to get a bad score anyway, but if they go one down it may help to score 100 instead of 50.' The other way to look at it is: 'If this is a silly contract and we defeat it, we will get a good score without doubling. But if it happens to be a lay-down, and easy to reach, to double will be disastrous.' This is really the sounder argument, but of course, towards the end of a pairs event, it is sometimes right to take chances and play for a 'top'.

2. And what is one to say about West's lead of the king of diamonds? I suppose, if you take partner's double seriously, there was some logic in the play, but the king of diamonds *looks* a good card and I'm not sure whether I would have dared to part with it. Oh well, if you can't be good, be lucky!

More Tales of Hoffman

by the same author

HOFFMAN ON PAIRS PLAY